SOLWAY GATE

By

Danny Thomas

Koinonia Associates, LLC
Knoxville, Tennessee

ISBN 978-1-60658-030-1

Published by:
Koinonia Associates
7809 Timber Glow Trail
Knoxville, TN 37938

To learn how you can become a published author, visit PublishwithKA.com
May 15, 2024

"Oftentimes fiction intrudes on facts, filtering
real-life events
through romance and adventure."

Wayne Flint

"…I had to identify how memory and history waltz in
step and sometimes strain to part,
to present not a lesson in history, of which there are
many, but a unique lesson in humanity."

Heather Morris

Introduction

Solway Gate is a work of fiction. All the incidents and dialogue and characters with the exception of some well-known historical figures are products of the author's imagination and, thus, are not to be construed as real. Where real-life historical figures appear, the situations, incidents, and dialogue concerning those persons are entirely fictional and are not intended to depict actual events or to change the entirely fictional nature of the work. In all other respects, any resemblance to persons living or dead is entirely coincidental.

Dedication

For Bonnie Albright Shoemaker, she who experienced firsthand the long aftermath of the Manhattan Project, she who cherishes the history of Anderson County, and she who uses a red ink pen to point out my mistakes, she who doesn't mind doing that, not one iota.

Also for Deb Kile Hotchkiss, whom I've known since I first started school, she who knows Oak Ridge far better than I do, she who chuckles at some of my sillier notions, and kindly sets me straight.

Acknowledgments

I am grateful to my daughter, Amanda Whalen, for helping me navigate through various tech issues and especially for her artful eye that shapes the cover of this book.

To Ray Smith and Keith McDaniel and their YouTube series, <u>Hidden History: Stories from the Secret City</u>, which celebrates the historical significance of Oak Ridge, just as does this book.

To Carol Brown who studies my rough drafts with a critic's aplomb, who sends me encouragement at every opportunity, and who promotes my books to anyone who can read.

And finally, to my better half, Cynthia, who serves as my beta reader, my confidante, and, if necessary, my fierce advocate, frequently encouraging me to "Work some more on this story. It's lacking something. I think you can do better. Now go back and get started on it."

That works for me. She makes all the difference.

Table of Contents

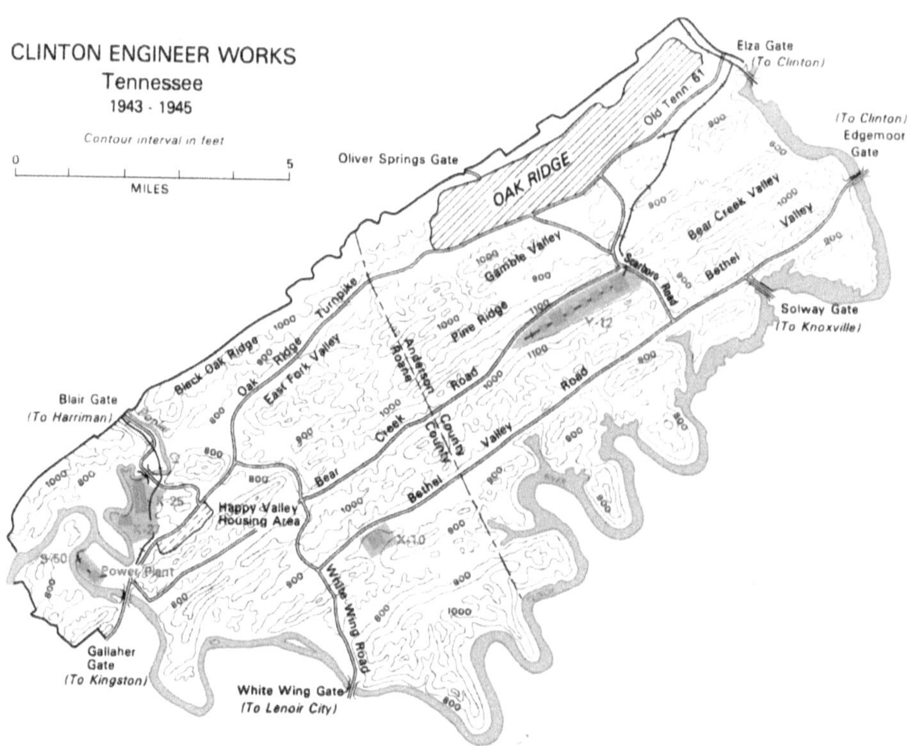

CLINTON ENGINEER WORKS
Tennessee
1943 - 1945
Contour interval in feet
0
5
MILES
Elza Gate
(To Clinton)
(To Clinton)
Edgemoor
Gate
Oliver Springs Gate
OAK RIDGE
Old Tenn. 61
Bear Creek Valley
Valley
Gamble Valley
Bethel
Scarboro Road
Solway Gate
(To Knoxville)
Pine Ridge
Y-12
Black Oak Ridge Turnpike
Oak Ridge
East Fork Valley
Anderson County
Roane County
Road
Road
Valley
Blair Gate
(To Harriman)
Bear Creek
Bethel
Happy Valley
Housing Area
Power Plant
X-10
White Wing Road
Gallaher
Gate
(To Kingston)
White Wing Gate
(To Lenoir City)

Minor Resident

Fourteen-year old Ronnie Woodson's first meeting with Mr. Buckley was in early March, 1944, and it was a downright strange encounter. The boy had taken the bus from Elza Gate to Solway Gate. Then he had walked across the languid Clinch River using the Solway Bridge to get across to Fairview Church where his father had told him he was to wait for the man.

Going around to the back door of the church, Ronnie wanted to see if the man was in there. He knocked. No answer. So he walked to the closest window and peered inside. Again nobody home. He studied his reflection, running his hand over his blond crewcut, noting the array of freckles across his cheeks and nose. He wished those freckles weren't so distinctive because the kids at school teased him about his freckles.

He backed up to see the whole picture, him standing there in his white T-shirt, blue jeans, and the new brogans Momma had bought him, still stiff and new. And there was the thermos he was carrying. Not his, but it was nice, blue with aluminum trim. He held it up to see what it looked like in the window, noting there wasn't much slosh inside it because it was nearly full. He couldn't help glancing down at the dog tag he wore on a lanyard around his neck. The small flat metal rectangle read "Ronald Woodson---Minor Resident---Food Service." It wasn't like the dog tags soldiers wore, but it always reminded him about the War, and how he was supposed to be wearing it all the time. Ronnie thought about the War every single day, and he liked thinking about it. He wanted to see the War up close somehow instead of just hearing and reading about it. He would have given anything to have been in that military hospital when General Patton slapped that guy, and he almost hoped that maybe some cannon or bomb had gone off at the bridge.

He stepped lively as he made his way a few yards into the backyard and waited sitting on one of the picnic tables, but had not really gotten settled before he was jolted by a loud explosion. The noise had come from about a hundred yards away, down near the bridge. At first he thought it was the enemy…Japs? Germans?… attacking the Solway Gate guards, trying to get into Clinton Engineer Works. But the longer he listened, the more he understood the noise must have been something else. This was no attack. There were no more loud reports interrupting the bright, warm afternoon. Everything had got quiet again.

The breeze brought a change in the traffic noise on the highway as automobiles were slowing and stopping on the gravel roadway. Ronnie couldn't actually see what had caused the commotion, but now he was hearing voices out on the road. He stood looking in the direction of the bridge and the Clinch River beyond, wondering if he should go see what had happened. Or did he need to wait for the man he was supposed to meet, that Mr. Buckley? He was the man Ronnie was supposed to give the thermos to.

His father, Earl, had told him what to do, holding up the thermos. "Mr. Buckley needs to see what we've got here, and that will help him decide if he's going to do business with us. As bad as things are these days with the War going on and all the rationing and shortages, we most definitely need Mr. Buckley's business. You remember that. Our store's about the only one left around here. Key's Store down in Robertsville, it's gone. Nash Copeland's place is gone. So is Freels' Crossroads Store. We're lucky Old Man Hill built his store outside of Elza, else we'd be gone, too. You do this like I tell you for the good of your Momma and sisters and brothers, your granma, and me and for your own good, too. You got that?"

"Yes, sir. I got that."

As he had ridden the bus Ronnie had peeked inside the thermos, sniffing at it, but not tasting it because his Dad had said, "This splo I'm making, you wouldn't like it, buddy. It's is for grown-ups, not for the whole world to know about. Like all the freight cars going into the CEW. This stuff is Top Secret."

Saying this, his father had handed Ronnie the thermos, adding, "Just deliver this to Mr. Buckley at Fairview Church, and come on back home, all right? Don't open the thermos. Don't mess with it. Just do what I tell you."

"Yes, sir, I'll do it. I promise."

But that promise had been broken before Ronnie even sat down at the church picnic table.

As Ronnie was recalling all this, it was becoming apparent there was some sort of problem on the highway. Traffic was stalled with cars backed up on this side of the road. On the other lane there were no cars heading up the hill toward Knoxville. He told himself, *Got to be a wreck.* He decided to go take a look. After all, he could always get back to the picnic table once he'd seen what kind of wreck it was. He walked around the front of the church. Soon he could see that a dark sedan had slid off the road and hit the concrete bridge abutment, wisps of steam still emanating from the crumpled hood. Several men were gathered around the wreck. Others farther up the hill were walking toward the bridge. Ronnie stood watching for a while as the crowd grew larger, then remembered the thermos in his hand, and decided to retrace his steps. He didn't want anybody to ask him about it. As he rounded the corner of the church he saw there was a small male, probably a teenager, sitting at the table, and he was flustered now because he was going to need to get the guy to leave. Dad wouldn't want anyone to be around when Mr. Buckley got there. That would not be good. Ronnie kept walking, thinking how to get the guy to leave the meeting place.

The guy was facing the other way so Ronnie couldn't see his face, but he saw that the fellow was about his same height, maybe a little taller, fairly slender, wearing blue jeans and a dark jacket. On his head, a worn and crumpled baseball cap. And he noticed the fellow's boots, work boots or maybe cowboy boots. Hard to tell from behind.

As Ronnie got up close where the fellow must have become aware of his approach, the guy didn't acknowledge his presence. Didn't even look in Ronnie's direction. Ronnie cleared his throat and said, "Hi."

"Hi yourself," was the reply. "You Ronnie Woodson?"

Ronnie was surprised to see how wrong he had been to think he was dealing with a teenager. The person before him was an adult male. In fact, he was not a young person at all, probably a laborer of some sort. His hands were calloused. He had a wiry appearance, a coarse, weathered look, needing a shave, and Ronnie estimated the man was older than his father.

"You're Ronnie, ain't you?" the man repeated. His crystal blue eyes studied Ronnie.

"Oh, yes, sir," Ronnie answered, holding his badge out to show the man. "Sorry. You Mr. Buckley?" There was no Identification Badge on him.

"That's right." He stretched out a hand. "Lemme see what's in there."

Ronnie handed over the thermos as Mr. Buckley patted the bench beside him. "Set down, buddy. This won't take long."

Ronnie did as told, unable to avoid watching as the man unscrewed the lid of the thermos. Sky blue with aluminum trim, the thermos was something Earl Woodson took good care of. Ronnie had been surprised that he had been given permission to carry it on the bus. Now he was anxious Mr. Buckley might drop it or damage it somehow.

Once the lid was off, Mr. Buckley peered inside, waved it around a bit, lifted it to sniff the contents just as Ronnie had done, and then he took a sip from it, closing his eyes briefly as he tasted. The man stared at him for a long moment, and Ronnie wondered what was going on. What did it taste like?

"Your dad's a smart feller," Mr. Buckley said, screwing the lid back on.

"How's that?" Ronnie said, thinking the man was right about his father, but wondering how Mr. Buckley knew this. He liked Mr. Buckley without knowing why.

"He's smart for sending his splo with you," Mr. Buckley said, grinning. "That's a nice touch. Guards didn't think you was anything special, I bet."

"You mean the guards here at Solway Gate?"

"I mean anywhere. The guards anywhere in the CEW wouldn't think you're carrying moonshine. When you go through a Security Checkpoint, they don't bother with you. Not with some kid. That's pretty good." He chuckled. "Nice to meet outside a church, too. A public place, but folks don't hang around in a church yard on a chilly afternoon."

Ronnie said, "Can I have the thermos back now?"

"Sure," Mr. Buckley said. "But I'll keep the splo."

"How you gonna do that? You gonna drink it all right here?"

"Nope," the man said, standing up. "Come on. I'll show you."

They walked across the road, crossing between cars stopped almost bumper to bumper on the road, and entered the Esso station where Mr. Buckley put a quarter on the counter and spoke to the old lady clerk, "We need a couple cokes."

She took his money, slid a nickel back across the counter, and said, "We got Nehi and Royal Crowns."

"That'll do," Mr. Buckley said.

He led Ronnie to the long red cooler under one of the front windows, lifted the lid, motioning Ronnie to make a selection. The boy slid his hand down into the cold water and brought out a dripping Grape Nehi.

"Git me one," the man said. They opened both Nehi's at a bottle opener set on the wall, heading outside to sit on a shaded bench facing the pumps and the road beyond. Buckley offered his drink to Ronnie. "You want this? I ain't gonna drink it."

"Huh?"

He shook the bottle. "You want this, or not?"

"Sure." Ronnie took the bottle, drank a swig, watching the people at the wreck. He set the bottle on his knee.

"Drink up. Drink up," Mr. Buckley said, impatiently.

"Huh?"

"I just need the bottle, buddy."

"Oh." Ronnie drank quickly, draining the purple carbonation after a few seconds before handing over the empty.

Carefully, the man poured the contents of the thermos into the empty Nehi bottle. When finished, he handed the thermos to Ronnie and took a generous sip of the clear liquid in the bottle.

"Umm hmm!" he said. "This will sell quick."

They sat in silence for a while, and Ronnie grew anxious just sitting while Mr. Buckley took an occasional sip. He swung his leg out and back, trying not to stare at Mr. Buckley, taking furtive sidelong glances now and then.

"I expect they'll get that wreck all sorted out pretty soon," Mr. Buckley said. "You want to go watch em?"

"Well, I guess I could," Ronnie answered. "I need to get back home, too. I'll catch the bus back to Elza Gate."

"You will if you can get past the wreck," Mr. Buckley said, standing. "I'll walk down there with you." He stuck the bottle in his jacket pocket.

When they got as close as possible, Mr. Buckley watched the people near the only apparent victim of the accident, a man laid out on the ground with a couple men kneeling by him. Somebody was wiping his face with a white handkerchief. His face looked pretty normal, generally unremarkable except for being abnormally pale. He wore a white dress shirt, green tie, and dark navy slacks. Ronnie thought he was somebody important, dressed as he was.

Mr. Buckley asked a man, "What happened here?"

"Don't know," was the answer. "Somebody said he passed out before he hit the bridge. They called the hospital. Ambulance on the way, but the guy's dead. Wasted trip."

Ronnie turned his attention back to the man on the ground. He didn't look like Ronnie thought a dead person should look. Ronnie thought any second he'd moan or move his hand a bit like somebody sleeping, slow to wake up. Thinking about that too long spooked Ronnie, and he turned away. This was the first dead person he'd ever seen up close.

People were milling around, several inspecting the sedan, which had hit the concrete bridge abutments and swung around so it extended into each lane. Just far enough to prevent traffic from moving in either direction.

"I expect this will get cleared up pretty quick," Mr. Buckley said.

Ronnie said, "Why do you say that?"

"The government won't stand for this mess holding up people getting to work," he said.

"Or getting home," a man said.

"Oh, government don't give a shit about that," Mr. Buckley said. "They just care about their own selves. About getting the job done. This road ain't gonna stay blocked for long."

Just then several cars pulled up on the far side of the wreck. A jeep was out front followed by a dark sedan and three trucks, each full of soldiers. The guys in the jeep quickly took over the scene, pushing onlookers back with, "Give us room here. Give us some room." The soldiers came up, and an officer directed them to move the wreck over to clear a lane. When they were through, an officer gave orders to start one-way traffic across the bridge, beginning with traffic entering the Federal Reservation.

Ronnie heard a soldier say, "Lt. Blankenship, how does this look?" The officer, a pretty young guy dressed better than the others. Pressed trousers, tie neat as a pin. He said," Give priority to this water truck. Let it through first."

The driver, a big, dark-skinned Negro, said, "Thank you kindly, sir. We thank you." The other Negroes in the truck's cab said nothing. Blankenship said, "Let all this lane across the bridge before you switch directions."

This didn't make the other lane happy, and one man spoke up, "What the hell is this? Ain 't you ever gonna let us go?"

"Not just yet. We're giving priority to people going to work first."

"Well, that's no goddam good," the man grumbled, his voice rising. "Let us through! Come on, come on. Who's in charge of you clowns?"

A big man dressed in khaki smiled and said, "That would be me." He had a barrel chest which was accentuated because he wore his pants so high. Ronnie thought his father would call the man "High Pockets." The man who was obviously the one in charge had wavy hair trimmed short on the side and brushed here and there with gray, and he wore a modest mustache more gray than dark. He gave the impression he was studying everything at Solway Bridge without worrying too much about questions being put to him.

The man complaining asked him, "Who're you anyway?"

The Lieutenant jumped in, explaining, "This is General Leslie Groves. Who're you?"

The Groves name apparently meant something to the complainer as he stopped talking, retreated a step or two, and muttered, "Nobody." And he wound his way back through the onlookers as the General said to an officer who had been in the car with him, "Do a quick assessment, Blankenship. Report soon as you can."

"Yes, sir."

Mr. Buckley tugged Ronnie's sleeve and circled around so they were behind a group of onlookers who had been herded off the road. They watched the soldiers continuing to manhandle the wreck toward the highway shoulder. Mr. Buckley seemed more interested in Lt. Blankenship than General Groves, which was opposite of Ronnie's interest. Ronnie drifted along the shoulder to keep the General in sight and earshot while Mr. Buckley tracked the Captain. In this way they lost one another for a few minutes. After a while someone tapped Ronnie on the shoulder. "Come on, boy," Mr. Buckley said. "We need to get back to the Esso."

Ronnie said, "I want to stay…."

"No, you ain't," Mr. Buckley said sharply. "We need to make ourself scarce."

Ronnie saw how agitated he was, so he went along with him. When they were a few steps away, he said, "What is it, Mr. Buckley? What you gonna tell me?"

"Let's set back down on that bench," the man said, glancing back over his shoulder. "Don't want nobody else around."

"Why?"

"Hush up," he said, walking quickly back up the hill.

Back on the bench Mr. Buckley said, "What did you learn?"

"Well, I don't know," Ronnie said. "Not much really."

"Did you hear the man's name that wrecked?"

"No, sir. I was mostly watching the General. You were closer to the Lieutenant and all the soldiers."

Mr. Buckley rubbed his mouth and chin and like he was deciding what to say. "They won't no skid marks. That's the first thing."

"So what does that mean?"

"Driver might have been drunk or passed out or something," Mr. Buckley said. "He hit the bridge going full speed. Now that the man's dead Porter's taking his own sweet time finishing up. I heard him tell somebody to bring up the 'girl-guy' thingamajig. You got any idee what that is?"

"A 'girl-and-a-guy?'"

"Naw," he said. "Not a 'girl-and-a guy.' It's just a 'girl-guy' thing. Or maybe the other way round. Guy-girl. And it might have something to do with cooking somehow."

"How do you mean?" Ronnie asked. "This doesn't make much sense. Not to me."

"Me neither," Mr. Buckley mumbled. He pulled the Nehi bottle out gazing across the road and sipped the splo. "Blankenship said they needed to find out how hot the wreck was." He shook his head, then turned to look directly at Ronnie. He held out the bottle. "You want some of this?"

"I…uh…I…."

Mr. Buckley handed it to him, saying, "I won't tell your Daddy. Just taste it. You don't have to gulp it all down neither. Leave the rest for me."

Ronnie took a swig, blinked as he took it in, handing the bottle back as the liquid burned down his throat, and he coughed.

"Good, ain't it?" Mr. Buckley grinned.

Ronnie sputtered again, nodding slowly as his companion chuckled quietly and took another pull from the bottle.

"How do you git that little badge you're wearing?" Mr. Buckley asked.

"I don't know," Ronnie said. "They give em to you if you're working in the CEW. Or if you have to go in to do business. Daddy gave me mine. He said to wear it all the time. You don't have one, do you?"

"Not yet, I don't," he answered. "But I'm gonna git another one soon."

They sat like that for a while as the traffic picked up in both directions.

Mr. Buckley said, "I heard Blankenship tell the General the man was dead before he wrecked. That really got Groves' attention. He said 'Shut it all down here. Close the bridge. Close the Solway Gate. Reroute traffic through Elza.' You shoulda seen Blankenship's face. He said, 'General, that will add at least forty-five minutes for some of these folks to make their destinations.' Groves didn't give a shit. He just said, 'It doesn't matter. We need to find out how Dr. Leman died. You take all the time you need investigating. I'll take the heat for anybody who complains about shutting down the Solway route.' Mr. Buckley shook his head back and forth. "Groves acts like he's Big Ass Pete."

The automobile was now completely off the road, and, although a soldier was still directing traffic, cars were moving almost normally going into CEW and coming out. In addition to the buses and automobiles lined up, long trailer trucks were scattered throughout the traffic. At one stretch Ronnie counted five trailer trucks in a row, a fact that seemed to impress Mr. Buckley, too.

The man said, "Everything's going into the CEW. Ain't nothing coming out."

"Is that good?" Ronnie asked.

"Could be," Mr. Buckley said. "They ain't exactly sharing whatever they're bringing in, are they? Bunch of foreigners and Yankees making money off us Tennesseans. And we ain't gitting shit."

"How's that?"

"I see you got some good brogans there," Mr. Buckley said, indicating Ronnie's shoes. "You're lucky."

"First new shoes I've had in a long time," the boy said. "Momma told Daddy I had to have them cause I'm growing so fast."

"Yeah," Mr. Buckley nodded. "You're lucky you can git em. Just about anything worth having these days is gitting rationed. Hardship is all most of us know these days. All for the damned War Effort. Good for all the soldiers in the war, but downright miserable hard on the rest of us."

"Momma says we all need to do our part," the boy said.

"Yup, but I'd like to have some say in what exactly my part is. Something more than just a say in it. A damned sight more. Oh, I know hardship is the natural condition nowadays. I know it, and it ain't going away any time soon…so I'm gonna do all I can to count on it. There's more than one way to make good use of hardship, buddy."

Ronnie said, "I don't follow."

"Hardship is good for the true bidness man," Mr. Buckley said. "And I aim to be one of the truest bidness men in CEW someday. If I can get me a job beyond the bidness me and you and your Daddy are doing."

"You don't work in the CEW now?"

"Nope," he said, staring across the road again. "But I will pretty soon. I promise you that. I'll be in there soon." Buckley winked at him and said, "Tell your Daddy we're ready to do bidness, him and me. You'll be doing some, too, I expect." And somehow this struck Buckley as funny. He clapped Ronnie on the back as his laughter turned uproarious. It took him a while to get it out of his system.

On the bus Ronnie thought a lot about Mr. Buckley, wondering mostly about the wreck and what had caused it. He tried not to think about the dead driver lying on the ground. He remembered Captain Porter and General Groves. As he got off the bus at the Elza Gate and was walking past his father's store the rest of the way home, he suddenly thought about tasting that splo, that moonshine, wondering could his father smell it on his breath.

One Faithful Week

I have run into this before. My struggle with the sin of pride. I find myself returning every night before I go to sleep to the events of my first week in command. Several times I've nearly spoken of it while on the phone with Grace, and she's tuned in to me so well that she has asked, "So can you tell me how your work's going? I hear some general excitement in your voice, but also a reticence to explain. I do wish you'd share with me, not only the good news, if there is any, but, of course, the rest of it, too. The bad as well as the good. I want to help and support you, even if it's only emotionally. I do wish we were together. You know that, Dick. Surely, you're aware of how much I miss you. How much Gwen misses you. I'm sure Richard would say the same thing."

In reply I often sat in silence, wondering how I could help her understand the breadth and depth of this work. She was aware I could never be specific. I'd never put her or the children in jeopardy by divulging Top Secret details. I wanted them safe from harassment if the unthinkable occurred, and enemies kidnapped them or simply invaded and discovered they were related to me. I probably over-reacted along those lines, keeping them uninformed and innocent of any information about the Clinton Engineer Works or the Manhattan Project, which surely must have been frustrating.

But that first week I'd been in charge back in September, 1942---that had been an auspicious week. One fateful week. Before I took command my predecessor, Jim Marshall, had been overly cautious. He dragged his feet. The preparation work that would lay the foundation for the Manhattan Project had languished for nearly three years. But when I was able to decide where the weapon would be built around Elza, Tennessee; and then wrangled that AAA priority rating; and pushed staff to purchase all the Belgian Congo ore, the biggest cache of uranium ore in the world---that was one very good week of work. I like Jim Marshall, but he simply wasn't doing what needed to be done.

So I was able to smile while talking on the phone with Grace. "Things are coming together rather well," I told her. "We've made good decisions about where to do the work. We won't have to worry about getting supplies, which could be good a hundred times over. But what might be the best news is we've found a critical ingredient for the project. Something absolutely critical, and we've taken it off the market. Nobody else can use it."

I must have let my enthusiasm show as I said all this because Grace seemed to take a long, deep breath without saying anything. Finally, she said, "I'm so glad for you, darling. It sounds like you've gotten off on the very best first step you could have hoped for." I heard the smile in her voice and could envision her sitting at the breakfast table aglow in her devoted happiness for me. It was a moment I returned to again and again every night when I was in bed reviewing my day. Grace at the breakfast table, smiling into the phone.

Quite a week.

Oak Ridge Hospital in 1944

Respite

In April, 1942, the radio was all about Lt. Colonel Jimmy Doolittle leading a squad of B-52's on a secret mission over Japan, bombing Tokyo and Yokohama. That raid was about the only good news the country had about the War, but it depressed me something awful because I wasn't going anywhere. I was home, tending cows, chickens, and hogs while my buddies at Jacksboro High were all joined up fighting Japs or Germans.

To make things worse, even though most guys had left town, I hadn't found myself a girlfriend. I just never knew what to say to a pretty girl. I was downright stupid that way. If I could just somehow get into the War, somehow do some good, that would do the trick. I'd be really something, and all the females would surely come looking for me.

Ma saw how pathetic I was, and after another six miserable weeks she said I could go. "Pa and me, we'll be all right. But, Roscoe Alvin Sturgis, you listen to me. Wherever you're assigned, you got to find out who's got the real say-so. It ain't always who you'd think. Ain't always the generals."

Pa was watering hogs when I found him. Sitting on a stump, he cut a plug of his chaw, and began preaching at me. "It ain't no silly game you'll be playing, buddy. Every mother's son has got to face life on his own, and you best get your mind right because your Ma and me, we won't be there to help you."

The next Monday I signed up at the LaFollette post office, caught a bus, and went to training in Ft. Jackson, South Carolina, where I got bossed by every fellow with a stripe on his shoulder. They had me marching everywhere, saluting everybody. I got sent to North Carolina for another few months at Ft. Bragg, which wasn't no picnic. I got wore down to a nub.

I didn't end up going to the fighting in France or Africa or the South Pacific. Instead, they sent me to something called the Clinton Engineer Works, just south of Jacksboro. I was assigned to the Military Police because I'm bigger than most. Mainly what I do is bear hug drunks from behind. Somebody else gets in their face, and I slink up from behind. I squeeze and squeeze so the air comes out of their lungs but can't get back in. I cracked a few fellows' ribs that way, but my sergeant doesn't mind that. "Serves 'em right for resisting," he says.

I didn't have no idea at all what the CEW was or what I'd be doing. It was a fluke that I got sent there, so close to home. I was able to see the folks a couple times, and I told them how homesick I was. But even so, I made it through bit by bit, which brings me here.

Since I left home I've made the best of my situation, and here it is September of '43. The War is still grinding away, God help us, and, besides Doolittle, the news ain't much good. Seems to me most everything about this CEW outfit looks temporary. And that's no good. One day you're in a tent. Next day they've thrown up dormitories for the whole unit. Then they move you out that very next day, and after that it's not as nice as yesterday. But there ain't no going back, is there?

I'm walking on eggs around Corporal Cavanaugh. His given name is Donald, but I'm not sure getting friendly with him's going to help. He's a corporal. I'm just a private. He's near thirty. I've just turned twenty. And he's been assigned to the CEW longer than me. Standing around five feet, seven, weighing maybe 130 pounds, Cavanaugh's a wiry, dark-haired, cheerless fellow who enjoys being in charge. I'd feel better working for an officer instead of a non com like Cavanaugh, but the CEW is just getting set up. New construction every day. Soldiers coming in on every train or bus. Our officer is supposed to show up this week. Maybe today.

I'm a head taller and forty pounds heavier than the Corporal, but he's one of those loud, little, fast-talking guys, so I turn away to watch our prisoner, a fellow dressed in a white shirt, dark slacks, and a dark tie. Seated alone at the table, the prisoner's calm as can be. Dr. Solomon Page is his name.

I ask myself, *What did this fellow Page do to land here?* He's a pale, skinny fellow with gentle brown eyes, dark, curly hair, and a big, old, lumpy nose. Seems nice enough to me.

"A Lieutenant Blankenship will be here soon," Cavanaugh tells Page. "He'll want to know your complete background, job duties, like that. So don't hold nothing back. You best answer our questions."

I figure *Cavanaugh might be somebody to learn from.* And I'm taking inventory around the room, noticing the windows have got bars across them. That fits with the door to the room, which is heavy and solid, like in a jail cell.

Page pipes up, "How many sessions will Lt. Blankenship have with me?"

Cavanaugh grumbles, "As many as he wants."

"I should return to the K-25 laboratory," Page says. "Our work must continue. We have sufficient equipment even though our facility is still under construction. But under these conditions, my team cannot make progress without me." He sounds old fashioned to me, formal and respectful.

Cavanaugh says, "Yeah we know, we know. You're a big shot. Sit tight, buddy. The Lieutenant will be here soon."

Not ten minutes later an officer walks in on us. This fellow's about Cavanaugh's size, but dressed neat, shoes polished bright, eyeglasses perched halfway down his nose. He says, "Dr. Page. I'm Lt. Robert Blankenship." He nods at Cavanaugh and me. "Gentlemen, I've read reports about you. We'll talk later." And he sits down across from Page, pulling papers from a leather brief case. He turns to us, "I'm going to talk with Dr. Page a while. Observe closely. I may need your assistance." He pats the file and turns back to Page. "Are you ready to proceed, Dr. Page?"

"I am indeed," Page says, but there's a wary look on his face. I'm a little surprised myself; Blankenship is so considerate. Or seems to be. He starts collecting basic information, noting subject's age, height, home address, education, work history. All of it routine, very thorough. Boring, really.

Page must think so, too. "I have waited here most of the afternoon. My colleagues need me." Then out of left field he says, "If I am to remain here merely biding time, I want to discuss the game of baseball."

Huh? I look to the Lieutenant, who says, "Baseball? My, oh, my!"

How will Blankenship handle this? I know how Cavanaugh would react. Cuss a blue streak. Deny the request flat out.

The Lieutenant's amused. He says, "I don't follow the game much, but I understand it's hard to go against the Yankees."

"I am partial to the St. Louis Cardinals," Page says. "I follow one of their outfielders closely, a promising second-year player."

Blankenship says, "You're more familiar with baseball players than I am. I'm not sure I can accommodate your request."

But I can. You bet your ass I can! I was a lights out pull hitter playing ball in Jacksboro, and I pull for the Yanks. Blankenship must be reading my mind. "Private Sturgis, you look like you want to say something. Are you a baseball fan? Corporal Cavanaugh, what about you?"

Cavanaugh scowls. "Not me, sir," like he'd die before picking up glove or bat.

I can't help but pipe right up, "I know baseball, Lieutenant. I mean, yeah. The Cardinals are World Champs. They're probably going to meet the Yankees in the World Series again this year."

Cogs start turning in the Lieutenant's head as he turns to Dr. Page. "I tell you what," he says. "I have appointments at the hospital. Corporal Cavanaugh's going to drive me over there. Private Sturgis remains here. You can talk baseball with Sturgis." Page looks astonished. I'm tickled pink. I glance at Cavanaugh, but he's not interested in what I think.

Blankenship and Cavanaugh go on down the hall. Page, he's calm again. "Private, do you recall last year's first game of the World Series?"

"Sure," I say. I figure I'm supposed to keep on doing like I'm doing. "Last season the Yanks won Game One."

Dr. Page says, "The Cardinals scored four runs in the bottom of the ninth to trail by three. With two outs they loaded the bases, bringing a rookie to the plate. Do you remember him?"

"You betcha," I say. "It was Stan Musial with that dainty, pigeon-toed batting stance of his. As funny as he looks at bat, he's one great hitter."

Page nods. "But Musial grounded out to end the game."

I'm puzzled that he wants to relive a loss. Page has got another odd look on his face. He says, "Are you aware Musial hails from Donora, Pennsylvania?"

"I've heard about Donora somewhere," I say, wracking my brain to remember. "Where was it?"

"I grew up in Donora," Page says proudly. "My parents have lived there nearly fifty years. My sister is there, too."

I say, "Oh, yeah. You mentioned Donora while the Lieutenant was questioning you. I remember now. Do you know Musial?"

"He is part of why I want to talk baseball. It is a favorite subject of mine. A refuge, you might say."

To me baseball is the absolute greatest game, and I guess Page can see how I feel from my expression, my close attention. I tell him, "I can't talk much about anything but baseball. I ain't otherwise qualified."

"I saw your face when the Lieutenant mentioned the Yankees," Page says. "They are dear to you. Am I correct?"

"Yeah, I'm a big, big Yankee fan."

"The Cardinals are most dear to me," he says, and, as I ponder his words, I figure him and me are baseball buddies. Seems to me he's as grateful about that as he can be, and I'm pretty glad myself. Happy to talk Yankees and Cardinals long as he wants. So that's how the rest of the afternoon goes. Page talks and talks about Musial, his eyes bright, Adam's apple wobbling up and down when he speaks, and all that helps me like him even more. He's a regular guy. A good guy.

"I want to listen to the radio broadcast this year," Page says. "Addie and I always listen to the game when I am home. She loves the Cardinals as much as I do."

"She your girl?"

"What?" he says. "Who? Addie? Oh, no. Well, perhaps she is. . .in a way. I care very much for her." His face, already flushed, seems burnished a little more. "Sweet Adeline is my sister."

"Little sister?"

"She is ten years younger than I. Seventeen last March."

Pretty soon baseball is taking us places we dearly love to go. We take joy reliving games gone by, every pitch. Every hit. The psychological duel between pitcher and batter. Every throw to first. Dust billowing up when someone slides into home. The umpire's call. All of it.

He says, "You are so large. Are you athletic?"

Nobody's asked me this before. Of course, I play ball. I'm a first ball/fast ball hitter. I tell Page about that walk off homer I hit up in Jellico. The day I went three for four.

Suddenly, I get a twitch like I've touched an electric wire. It's after five o'clock, and Cavanaugh's not back. *Have I missed something?* I don't let on to

Page, but I'm anxious about how we've lollygagged the afternoon away.

When Cavanaugh finally gets back, he's not perturbed like he was when him and Blankenship left. Something's come up. I can tell by the way he looks, the way he steps up to Dr. Page, no longer hostile, just business-like. "Doc," he says. "We got a change of plans. Sturgis is to report to the Lieutenant over at the hospital. I'll be here with you. The Lieutenant, he'll see you tomorrow."

Page is none too sure about this. "At the hospital?"

"That's right," Cavanaugh says, turning to me. "Sturgis, he wants you to drive over there." He hands me the jeep key. "Go to the front desk. They'll direct you to where Blankenship's set up." I make for the door, but Cavanaugh says, "Hup, hup, hup, boy! I need the key to this room." He's got his hand out, impatient. I feel like a dolt. I hand over the key, and Cavanaugh's got a wrinkled forehead, like he's got more news for me, but don't really want to tell me. He walks me down the hall out of Page's hearing where he fesses up. "Let me explain something," he says. "They had some funny business at the hospital today."

"A goof ball almost killed hisself up on the second floor. He was a carpenter repairing a picture window in one of the end rooms. Slipped and broke through the glass. Cut hisself pretty bad. Lost a lot of blood. They've roped off the window, but some durn fool still might trip out the window onto all that rebar down below." He glances back at the door to Page's room. "If you end up with Page on that floor, watch him close."

"What are you saying?"

"I'm saying when crazy shows up, shit happens. Hazards like all that broken glass make me skittish." His face seems sincere like he's trying to help me. *But what if he's trying to pull something on me? I got to watch out. Got to be careful with Cavanaugh.*

The hospital is a substantial, three-story, wooden structure set up onto a ridge. At the front desk they point me upstairs to room 317 where I locate Blankenship in his shirtsleeves, tie loose at his collar. With blinds drawn the room is quiet and not so bright as the hallway, and there's an antiseptic aroma of alcohol in the air. There's three beds with a man laid out in each one. Blankenship motions me back out of the room, and once we're out of earshot, he says, "These men were in the K-25 accident."

"Sir," I say, "I don't have no idea what you're talking about."

"Dr. Page needs to help us understand what went wrong at one of the plants here. A place called K-25. Horrific accident. They were working with corrosive chemicals. We don't know yet if these fellows inhaled toxic gas. Three men got horribly burned, we know that. Two are comatose. The other man---named G. W. Woody---his throat is blistered so he can't talk. Not a word." Blankenship lays a hand on my shoulder. "We could end up losing all three of them."

I ask him, "Is corrosive some kind of poison?"

"Anything that's corrosive can eat away something else. Dissolve it, melt it." He's still watching me, trying to see if I understand, and it feels good that he does that. Everywhere you go in the CEW it's "Keep your mouth shut. Don't give away any secrets." But maybe Blankenship's special.

"These guys officers then?"

"Woody, Long, and Grubb are civilian contractors at K-25 working for Carbide," he says. "Federal jobs."

Nurses come in, seeing to each patient, checking charts, straightening blankets, studying their patients' breathing, their color, not speaking to us. After they leave one bed I venture closer, studying the man there, silent, all laid out: Gerald Long——-mustache, receding hairline, gray at the temples. He's got clear plastic mask over his nose and mouth, receiving oxygen, breathing shallow. He doesn't look good.

The next guy looks younger. Elvin Grubb, long face, high cheekbones. A weeping bandage on his neck. His breathing is labored, too, even with oxygen. I'd rather be with Page talking about Stan Musial. Chemicals blistering your throat, that's not my thing.

In the third bed I find Woody's awake. Slender, almost gaunt. His eyes meet mine, and he lifts a finger in acknowledgement, but it looks like he's not got energy to do much else. Hurting pretty bad, I figure. He licks his lips, and there's a dab of blood there on his mouth. I locate a wash cloth, using it to wipe his mouth, whispering, "You all right?"

Woody blinks again, barely shaking his head. *No, not all right.*

Later Blankenship and me go down the hall to the end room that's mostly windows—- some kind of sunroom. "Tell me about your conversation with Dr. Page," he says. So I take him through everything about Donora, Musial, and last year's Series. I'm quoting Page's actual words as much as I can, but I'm not real good at that. Now and then Blankenship prompts me with, "Did he bring that up, or did you?'" I had thought Blankenship would merely tolerate talk about baseball, not really taking much interest in it, but I was wrong. He's thinking of Page, not exactly coddling him, but trying to understand why he's so focused on the game of baseball instead of the fiasco at K-25. I want to know about that too.

"Did you pick up anything about their parents? It would be good if we could persuade a family member to get him talking."

I shut my eyes to think, and I remember how I'd thought maybe I'd done something wrong just asking Page how old Adeline is. Finally, Blankenship says, "Page has been sent here to develop a new kind of weapon. It puzzles me why he wasn't injured like the others. Something doesn't fit."

"Page can keep the accidents from happening again? Is that what you're saying?"

Blankenship stares off into space. "Page has high-level expertise in a special field of physics and chemistry. We think he can tell us what went wrong."

"But, sir, it sounds like you're not telling me something. Why is this K-25 thing so important? It's just three guys got hurt." Instantly, I regret saying that. Blankenship can tell me anything. Or nothing. Whatever he wants. The Lieutenant's quiet for a while, which worries me. *I got to learn to shut up.*

But Blankenship says, "Sturgis, I'm not constrained like other commanding officers. I've presented my proposal to my superiors, and they didn't care for it. But General Groves liked my idea and overruled them. He's chosen not to involve the Inspector General's office just yet. Normally, the IG investigates, but apparently not this time. The big deal is how much of this new chemical is required. The Brass want enough to stop Tojo and Hitler dead in their tracks before they do it to us. The General actually said, 'Gentlemen, we don't have time to try something, then give it up, and start over. We're going to try everything all at once.' General Groves has given me free rein. So tell me, what could be going on with our Dr. Page?"

In a flash out of the blue, I get an inkling.

"Tell me more about the sister," I say.

"As a matter of fact, Cavanaugh's working on that," Blankenship says. "I've told him to go ahead. We need to know more about the sister. His parents, too. I'm expecting a call from Donora at 2100 hours tonight."

I'm a little perturbed about whatever Cavanaugh's doing. I'd like to know what his idea is. I shouldn't, but I can't keep from blurting out, "It makes me think Page is hiding from something terrible by sticking to the game of baseball."

Blankenship nods. Somebody has brought in one of the Knoxville papers, which Blankenship tosses my way. "Go ahead, Private. But save it for me. I've got to think some more about our Dr. Page."

I never was one to pore over a newspaper, but I take my time browsing through the *Sentinel,* noting that the news from Europe still sounds grim. The Nazis have put down an uprising in the Warsaw Ghetto in Poland, killing thousands of Jews. Seems like every bit of good news we get there's worse news following along behind, leaving us adrift and asunder.

Blankenship is antsy, leaving the table twice while we're eating. When he comes back the second time, he says, "Grubb's dead. Never regained consciousness. Long seems to be doing a little better. Woody's stable."

The orderly pops his head in the door. "Lieutenant, you got a phone call down at the nurse's station. Long distance."

Blankenship bolts out the door, and I pick up speed with knife and fork, trying to finish the meal before he gets back. The call might not be important, but then again. . . .When Blankenship returns, he doesn't even sit down. "There's been an auto accident in Donora. Page's mother has a broken ankle." He shakes his head solemnly. "His father was pretty shaken up. He didn't make much sense over the phone. Asked a neighbor to finish the call. Let's go see Woody."

As we're going down the hall Blankenship pulls out a sheet from the folder. In a shaky scribble it reads *LUBE FIRE.* I'm looking it over as we're heading out the door. *What the hell is this?* I'm thinking. But I don't say it.

Blankenship says, "Woody wrote this. It's all he could manage. Then he slept."

"What's it mean?"

"It's about the accident," he says. "And, if he's strong enough, we may get answers we need."

"What're we going to do?" I say, and the Lieutenant takes a few minutes to lay it all out for me. When he's finished, I'm thinking, *This might just work.*

He nods. "We need Cavanaugh to be there, too. I'll go call him. Fill him in."

The Lieutenant leaves, and I check on Woody, his eyes popping open before I get close. It's like he'd been listening to us plan, getting himself ready. I place my hand on his mattress, careful not to touch him, although I feel like patting him on the shoulder to encourage him, maybe buck up his spirits. I'm not sure how to help him, but I tell him, "The Lieutenant's had a brainstorm. About helping you. He'll be here soon."

I can't read Woody's face. When Blankenship comes in, he moves a chair over to Woody's bed and says, "G.W., I hope you're feeling a little better. I hope you've had some rest."

Woody seems to come undone hearing this. Wearily, he gestures toward his mouth, shaking his finger across his lips, which I take for, *No good. Can't talk.* We're the three of us just staring at each other. One of us is thinking, thinking, thinking. One of us is hurting. One of us has no clue what happens next.

Blankenship comes up for air first. "Grubb and Long were hurt worst, and Page wasn't hurt at all." He inches up close to Woody. "Was he out of the room?"

Woody blinks very slowly and deliberately, which tells me what Blankenship has set up to communicate with the injured man. One blink means *Yes.* Two means *No.*

"You and Page were in the room," Blankenship says. "But you two weren't close to the pipe, right?"

Two blinks.

"No?" He looks to me. Then back to Woody. He says, "I'm stuck. That wasn't what I was hoping for. Let me think."

Woody lets out a long breath, closing his eyes. Blankenship and I move back out into the hall, and he says, "Did you follow that?"

"I think so," I say. "If this new stuff for piping as dangerous as you say, how could Page escape it when the others didn't?"

Blankenship's quiet a while, scribbling on his note pad. "Let's go back."

We find Woody's asleep again, so we move back into the hall. The Lieutenant says, "Let's get some rest, too. I'll bed down in the lounge tonight. You go back to your quarters, get some shut-eye. Be back here at 0600. Where are you billeted?"

I don't want to hear this. We can't stop now, but that's not what I say. I just say,"Rutland Hall. Down by the Central Bus Terminal."

I drive through fog to Rutland, and my eyes are shut soon as my head hits the pillow. Next morning I'm up too early. Can't help it. Nerves, I guess. I'm back at the hospital five minutes ahead of schedule. Blankenship's got a worn out look about him. He says, "Around 0300 Woody managed to write a bit, giving more details. When sparks started flying, Page yanked his lab coat over his face. Held his breath."

"So Page was right there with them?"

"Right," the Lieutenant says. "Woody was able to talk for about five minutes last night. Mostly just a hoarse whisper, but he says Page was hesitant to apply oil as a lubricant, but the pipe wasn't fitting like it should. But oil dripped on the pipe, just two or three drops. Right away they heard a sizzle, and there was a bitter, acrid aroma. Sparks flew everywhere, and Long and Grubb had gaping holes burned through their lab coats. Long was hit pretty bad in the neck." It's like somebody used a red hot poker on him.

"But Woody and Page weren't hit?"

Blankenship says, "Woody got hit, but Page took a couple steps back, and that made all the difference, but still he blames himself. Woody was telling me about that, but he overdid it. His voice gave out again. I asked more questions, but after a while he just ran out of gas."

"But he said Page blames himself? For not getting scalded?"

"Page hadn't got through to the men about what could happen if oil contacted new pipe. Woody says Page did warn them. Several times. Things went wrong just that one time."

Blankenship says, "The doctor says Woody's getting better, but the personnel here at the hospital haven't seen anything quite like what the burned men are dealing with. That leaves us facing something brand new and deadly"

That last little tidbit sinks into my brain, and I'm stymied.

Blankenship says, "Page's sister should be here about 1300 hours. Cavanaugh's collecting her in Knoxville." I'm more than a little curious about Adeline Page. Maybe he counts on her, relies on her. Or maybe it's the other way around: she mostly relies on him. After all, he's older.

Blankenship says, "Listen. Just talk baseball with him, but, for goodness sake, if he brings up the sparks and the oil, listen close. We need to know what he knows. Since the accident K-25 has ground to a halt."

My mind is trying to catch up on all this sparking chemistry and, I guess maybe Adeline, too. I'm just going to stick to baseball, if I can. Wouldn't know what to say to scientist or female. Stupid and clumsy either way.

By 0700 hours I'm back with Dr. Page, talking about Game Two of last year's World Series, which the Cards had won, 4 to 3. St. Louis won Game Three, 2 to 0. And Game Four, 9 to 6, leaving them one win away from winning the Series. I'm expecting Page to rush into reliving Game Five, but he stops, staring off into the distance instead of at me, and I don't get it. What's he waiting for?

Then I can see that he wants to keep thinking and talking about the '42 Series. As if all the talking we've already done never happened. The corrosive chemicals, the sparking pipe--- that's not my area. My best area is on a baseball diamond, playing the game. Not life or death. Just a game. So Page and me chew the fat about last year's World Series. We're back at Game One again. I come to realize what our conversation really is, is simpler and easier than the things going on at K-25. Everything I'm learning about this place is deep, and to me it looks like it has more secrets than I can count.

Abruptly, Cavanaugh's at the door. "Sturgis, come with me." Not acknowledging Dr. Page.

We're heading down the hall, and I say, "Where we headed?"

"Blankenship will say." Cavanaugh's back to his surly self again. I need to tiptoe around him. Not take it personal. He's not the one to learn from.

Blankenship's there in the sunroom with two others, one a short, animated fellow who's older, maybe 55 or 60, one of those red headed leprechauns with close cut hair, bright and friendly. There's a female next to him, but he's blocking my view, and I don't want to be obvious looking her over. After a little bit I glimpse long auburn hair and a navy blue dress with white polka dots. Long legs. Nice.

Blankenship handles introductions. "Miss Page, Mr. Meshak, this is Private Sturgis. He's spent considerable time with Dr. Page lately."

My heart does a little flip flop. This is her, Adeline Page---peaches and cream complexion, soft, brown eyes, high cheekbones. If her hair were darker, she'd be another Hedy Lamarr. There's something else about her. I can't decide what it is. I'm not sure what to make of Adeline Page.

Mr. Meshak breaks the spell. "Private Sturgis, can you tell me? Has Solomon talked about Stan Musial? Where we come from Stan's the talk of the town."

"Yes, sir," I say. "We've been all through the '42 Series, more than once actually. We've been talking about every little thing that happened. Every game."

Adeline chimes in. "Stan's batting average last year was .314. He had 10 home runs. This year his average is nearly .350." She's beaming at me.

She's ready to say more, but Blankenship says, "Please excuse Private Sturgis and me a few moments." Adeline's face is aglow. She's got a hold on me. *Or am I just goofy about her?*

In the hall the Lieutenant faces me. "Did you make any progress with Page? Any insight into the K-25 accident?"

"No, sir. Nothing new. He's just going over last year's Series again, retelling the story about how the

Cards ended up winning the whole thing. I think he enjoys the retelling for its own sake."

Blankenship sighs. "I was afraid of that. The technicians at K-25 are skittish about the new pipes. Oiling them is obviously out of the question, but now the scientists are considering graphite, which is subject to electrical charging. Much too volatile. We don't have the luxury of time. The whole effort might get scrapped, and Groves would not be happy about that."

"So," I say, "I guess we're in a hurry."

Blankenship gives me a side-eye look. "Big hurry. Biggest hurry you got. Let me make it clear, Private. If we lose, Groves doesn't want it to be because we didn't try everything we could come up with."

I wish I could help. Wish I could do more than baseball.

Mr. Meshak comes out into the hall, saying, "I need to use a bathroom."

"Three doors down on the left," Blankenship says, and Meshak says, "Lieutenant, can we talk some before I go back to Adeline?"

Blankenship says, "Sure." He turns to me. "Go keep Miss Page company."

So I head back to Adeline, my pulse quickening as I get to the doorway. When I enter the room, I'm thinking she'll be gazing out the window. Getting her bearings. Settling in. But there she sits, facing the doorway, just waiting on me.

"Miss Page," I say. "I've been sent to stay with you until Mr. Meshak gets back."

She cocks her head inquisitively. I decide to let her talk first. Just follow her lead. See where she wants to go. I try not to stare, but it's hard not to. The silence is not so easy to handle, but I'm trying. *I'd love to break the ice somehow. Not too sure how to go about it.*

"Did you know Stan used to be a pitcher?" she says.

"What?" I say. "No, I didn't know that."

She smiles. "Stan was a darn good pitcher," she says. "But he hurt his arm, and they said, 'Go play in the outfield.' So that's what he does now."

I'm wondering if she's chosen this topic to make it easy for me? Adeline Page is like a beautiful flower, and here I am tromping through the weeds, and I'm wondering if I've already missed something she's said. I'm keenly aware of her scent, something clean and flowery at the same time. Gardenias? Her face is just a couple of feet away. Part of me wants to step closer, but I don't budge. I keep a straight face, not knowing if I should smile or what. I feel myself slipping over the edge for Sweet Adeline. Any slender note of invitation in her voice would bring me to my knees. She's got a little handhold on my heart, that's for sure.

We talk baseball a while, and she really knows her stuff. Meshak joins us, and I can see how Adeline trusts him. I like him myself. I think Blankenship is happy with him, too, but I'm still in the dark about a lot of things. The Lieutenant comes back in, and Meshak says, "Please sit, gentlemen, and I'll explain."

He glances at her face, but mostly he's making eye contact with the Lieutenant and me. Meshak doesn't exactly say it, but I'm getting the message how special Adeline Page is. Not like anyone else I've ever known. Beautiful? Yes. A head for details? Yes. Like the rest of us? No. Just the same, I'd love to have her sitting in the bleachers, pulling for me.

Meshak says, "My wife, Greta, and I live two houses down from the Pages on Dorset Street on the west side of Donora. Millie and Reggie do Sunday School with us at First Presbyterian. Greta and I are Adeline's godparents.

"But Solomon is different. Always has been. He's never been much interested in church. Oh, he'd go with the family regular as clockwork. Even sang in the Youth Choir. Addie did, too." He halts to look at me. "But you could tell Solly's mind is on academics. Once he reads something all the facts are collected and sorted in his brain. That served him well at William and Mary and subsequently at University of Chicago. The family was real proud of him."

Lieutenant Blankenship has been taking it all in, staring at his shoes until this last comment, which causes him to sit upright.

"Until what?" Blankenship says." You're using the past tense. 'The family *was* proud of him. Not *is* proud of him."

"You know, I probably shouldn't have brought it up," Meshak says. "You probably stand a better chance of answering that question. I mean, something happened here, didn't it? That's why you wanted Millie and Reggie to come down here, isn't it?"

Blankenship says, "I was hoping they could fill in some blanks for us. And when you said was instead of is, I thought…well, I don't know what I thought. I was hoping maybe we can get through to Dr. Page so he'll open up to us. I'm trying not to strong arm him. The Inspector General would throw the book at him, but Dr. Page might just clam up totally if we go that way."

Meshak pats Adeline on the shoulder, saying, "So that's why you arranged for Addie to substitute for Millie and Reggie, isn't it?"

Blankenship nods. "That's right. Dr. Page witnessed an industrial accident here resulting in serious injuries and one death. We believe he knows more about it than he's told us."

Meshak looks to us with a finger to his lips. "Addie," he says softly, "why don't you lie down a while? You didn't get much rest on the train."

Wearily, she murmurs. "I couldn't sleep while we were on the train." She looks ready to sleep right there in the chair. Blankenship has me take her down to the nurse's station to get her settled into a room. By the time I get back, he's already talking about when the Pages had their auto accident. Two days ago.

"Reggie wasn't actually injured. Not that you'd notice," Meshak says. "But he's a little too heavy and doesn't get much exercise. Usually, it's Millie waiting on him. But here she is with a bad break of her right ankle, plus she may have had a concussion. Reggie told me on the phone she wasn't making much sense before the ambulance arrived. He was shaken up about her. Probably still is."

"Let me get things straight," Blankenship says. "You're neighbors with the Pages. Attend the same church. Do you work with Mr. Page at the mill?"

Meshak chuckles. "Heavens, no. I'm retired. Taught math at the high school thirty-one years. Greta and I are very close to the Pages. Adeline and Solly call us Aunt Greta and Uncle Paul."

"Do you know Stan Musial?" I ask.

Another chuckle. "Sure do. He took geometry under me. Very good at geometry. Not so good in algebra. B-minus or C-plus."

We run through stories about Musial a while. He was a bright star on the baseball team. Played nearly every position flawlessly. We're just talking and talking until Blankenship pulls us back to Solomon Page.

Meshak says, "Solly preferred mathematics and science. He's a whiz at applying principles he's learned in ways other people can't imagine. I knew he'd end up in science, either chemistry or physics."

"Maybe both," Blankenship says. And we're quiet a while, Meshak apparently waiting for the Lieutenant's questions, Blankenship deciding where to begin, and me trying to predict what comes next, wondering if it's something I'll be able to recognize and if I should have seen it myself.

A guy in carpenter's coveralls breaks the spell, bustling through the door carrying a tool box, struggling with a sheet of plywood probably four feet square. "Where's the broken window?" he says.

"The floor below," Blankenship says. The guy lets out a huff, rolling his eyes in exasperation, shoving the plywood against the wall so that the door's ajar. "These doors lock automatically, if you don't chock them open," he says. "It'll save me time if I can leave it like this." He chocks the door open with a shim. "Won't have to walk back through security."

"Nope," Blankenship says. "This floor is secure. No short cuts."

The carpenter huffs again. "They told me top floor," he says.

"Down a floor," Blankenship says with a little temper in his voice. "Get a move on."

The guy goes back out, and Blankenship tells me, "Go see the nurses. Tell them no one comes up here without my say-so." So I do that. When I get back, the Lieutenant's asking Meshak, "Was Dr. Page liked by his classmates? Was he a leader? Did you ever see him in a tight situation? Under pressure?" We're seated at a round table, and Meshak pushes his chair back a little, slides down in his seat, sticking his legs out, crossing his feet at the ankles.

"I hate it's come to this," he says ruefully. "At the Donora Hospital I talked privately with Reggie. He was fretful and bewildered when the Army officers interviewed him right there at the emergency room and wasn't able to be much help. Millie was hurting, but she seemed sharp as always."

The Lieutenant peers across the table, "So can we cut to the chase, Mr. Meshak? Can you help us understand Dr. Solomon Page? Or not?"

Meshak smiles briefly, nodding several times. "Solly was well liked at Donora High. He wasn't a standout athletically. Wasn't in the band or the drama club, but students knew, if you had trouble with a class, he could explain things in a way that wasn't judgmental. Not like a teacher, more like a trusted friend. He tutored a few who really needed help, and word got around about him."

Blankenship interrupts. "Was he a rule follower? Or did he cut corners?"

"No, he was a straight shooter. A good role model for everyone, students and adults alike."

Blankenship says, "You haven't talked about him under pressure when things got tense. Did that ever happen to him in Donora? What about in college? Do you know anything about that?"

"I never saw it," Meshak says.

It's quiet a while, and it seems to me something's been left unsaid. Blankenship shifts his eyes from Meshak, making eye contact with me, and he must see my concern. "What's on your mind, Private?"

"I don't think we really got an answer to your question, Lieutenant." I turn to Meshak. "Maybe you didn't see it, but maybe you know about it." I stare at this funny little man who I liked the first moment I laid eyes on him, but he's not smiling now.

"Solly's always been under pressure," he says. "Ever since Adeline was a toddler."

Blankenship says, "He's what? Ten years older than his sister?"

"Let me go at it another way," he says. "Addie was an extremely small infant, precious and lovely right from the start. Photogenic, you know. But she was quiet, unusually so. She didn't say anything. At all."

Blankenship says, "I don't understand."

Meshak rises from his chair. "Is it all right if I move around as I talk? I think better that way."

The Lieutenant waves a hand. "Sure. Go ahead." Meshak paces to the window and back, talking as he goes.

"Reggie noticed it first, playing with the baby, just as he had done when Solly was that age. He'd sing and laugh with her, cuddle her, but when Addie was about twenty months old he told me, 'I'm worried about her. She understands us, but she doesn't answer back. Doesn't say anything. At 15 months Solly was chattering away, talking a mile a minute, but not a peep from his little sister.'"

"I wasn't convinced there was a real problem. I told Reggie 'Every child is different.' But Reggie was right. She understood what she heard, but, other than grunts and squeals and the occasional whine, she didn't utilize language the way other children do. They checked her hearing early on, but that wasn't it.

"Until the evening of her third birthday when Millie and Reggie were sitting in their dining room and heard a crash from the kitchen. They rushed in to investigate. Millie said, 'What was that noise?' And there was little Addie, who said, 'Coffee maker.' Her first intelligible words. Millie and Reggie were stunned. From that moment on, Millie and Reggie focused not on her previous silences but on positive aspects of their daughter's personality, even though it was undoubtedly a totally different story than older brother's.

"Addie has an amazing memory. She can quote lines she's read weeks or months previous. She sings lyrics of any song she's ever heard, and with perfect pitch. She gets upset sometimes so bad nobody else but her brother can calm her. She loves him. Trusts him. And he loves her back."

Blankenship says, "But they get along, right? Two peas in a pod."

Meshak frowns. "Not really. About the only thing they agree on is Stan Musial. I'll hear them bickering, usually it's Addie who's loudest, and then Solly asks something like, 'How did Stan do against the Phillies?' And they're . . .well, they're...Addie Page is extraordinary is all I'm saying. Beautiful, but not always aware of others. Never had a serious boyfriend.

No real close girlfriends her own age. Greta thinks she might turn out to be an old maid."

That hurts to think of her being all alone like that.

Meshak wanders toward the door. He looks down the hall toward the room where she's napping. In a low voice, Meshak explains, "This trip is Addie's best chance to repay her brother.

"There were some tears. More than once she broke down sobbing. I thought maybe we'd have to put her in the hospital, too. I didn't know what to do. Finally, I gave Addie a big hug, telling her, 'Greta and I will help you any way we can.'

"She said, 'Uncle Paul, will you come with me?' The more she talked about it, the better we all felt about it."

Again Blankenship is nodding. "And we don't have any idea how Dr. Page will react to his sister's arrival. Or to yours, Mr. Meshak. We need to assure him his parents are properly cared for. But his sister is here pleading for him to help us understand the explosion. So far, he's refused to talk about it."

The door to Adeline's room opens, and she heads our way. I go to meet her, and she gives me a shy smile as my heart does that little flip over. Even with her hair slightly askew, for me she's just right. She grasps my hand a half-second while passing me, headed to Meshak.

"We've not told him about you," Blankenship says. "But seeing Mr. Meshak here ought to help. He might worry about his parents. He might get stressed, might overreact." He turns to us, then back to Adeline. "Miss Page, you and Mr. Meshak need to be prepared to calm his fears, if he has any. This floor will be secured, locked down tight. Once he's informed about his parents we need to talk about K-25. He was the only person in the room who escaped injury."

Then she looks at me, and I say, "Why don't you sit down?"

"Because I don't want to," she says, sharp and petulant with me. But to me she looks like she should sit. Meshak pushes a chair out for her. Reluctantly, she takes it.

Blankenship says, "Who's best to persuade him to answer questions?"

It's quiet while everybody works through that. Nurses are down at the far end of the hall. I hear their voices.

"Let Addie decide," Meshak tells Blankenship. "And I guess it needs to be quick. How much time do we have?"

"It's 1335 now. Let's bring Dr. Page up here at 1400 hours."

Blankenship says, "I'm going down to second floor to make sure 1400 hours will work."

After the Lieutenant's gone I gravitate to the window at the end of the hall. Building materials, apparently delivered yesterday, piled high in the parking lot. Hammering is underway on the floor below us. Voices now and then. The business down there is a long way from what we're about. I wish I was doing the hammering instead of wrestling with what we're in the middle of. I'd like to be outside, come rain or shine. Maybe in the outfield or down at third base, waiting for the ump to holler, "Play ball!" But, of course, if I wasn't in this mess, I wouldn't know Adeline Page.

I take a turn in the closest bathroom, then washing my hands I hear a ruckus out in the hall. Echoing vibrations of someone rushing up the stairs. Shouting down the hall. I push the door open an inch or two, and there's two MP's in combat stance, batons ready.

What the hell?

An MP says, "Drop it, buddy!" Not talking to me. To someone I can't see on the other side of the door.

I hear Meshak's voice. Just out of my view. He says, "Whoa, whoa, whoa! Do you really want to do that?"

Dr. Page is on the other side of the door, shouting everybody down. "Leave me alone. That is all I want. To be left alone."

Adeline steps up. "Solly, wait. Uncle Paul and me need to tell you some things. Mother and Father are in the hospital."

Meshak says, "They're all right, Solly. The doctors are just being careful. We all need to do that, don't we?"

Page must be stuck on what's coming at him. I have no clue, really.

Adeline steps closer. "Uncle Paul's all right. Please put the hammer down."

"It helps me," Page says. And that does it for me. I got to see what's going on. So I sidle out from behind the door.

Page flinches. Then he waves the hammer, turning his back on me. Like I don't matter.

Again he yells, "Leave me alone!"

Instinctively, I bear hug him from behind, forcing his arms down to his waist. The hammer clatters to the floor as the MP's close in and take over, cuffing his hands behind his back.

Blankenship arrives, a little out of breath. "What's going on?"

Page's looks all done in, like he doesn't care what happens next. His gaze drifts down to the floor.

Adeline is teary, cheeks flushed and glistening, keening like an animal caught in a trap, which agitates the MP's. "Ma'am, ma'am, don't do that. Back away, ma'am."

Meshak says, "She's his sister. She can help, if you let her."

The tallest MP, a Sergeant Chatwood, big as I am with a blond crew cut, he bristles and grumbles until Blankenship intervenes. "It's all right, Sergeant. I take responsibility."

"Your call, sir."

"Send someone to second floor," Blankenship says. "Check on Cavanaugh."

I haven't thought about Cavanaugh, focusing just on Page. Blankenship moves so he's out in front of us. He says, "Sergeant, give me a few minutes with Dr. Page. Then you can have him." He glances at me. "One more thing: Private Sturgis will attend to Dr. Page while he's in custody wherever we put him. Are we clear on this?"

Chatwood barks, "Yes, sir."

An MP shows up with Cavanaugh who's favoring his left arm. He's wincing with each step. He speaks directly to Blankenship, but obviously his excuse is to be public. "I saw the door to the stairwell had been chocked open, went to shut it, and saw Page heading up the stairs, so I followed him. Somehow he got hold of a hammer, and when he whirled around, the hammer almost brained me. I stepped back, but the step wasn't where I thought it would be. I ended up taking a header down half a flight. This arm," he says, lifting it gingerly, "feels broke."

Adeline sees Page yawn, and it sets her off. "What's got into you, Solly? What's wrong with you?"

The Lieutenant says, "Cavanaugh, go get looked at. Right now we're going to talk with Dr. Page." Blankenship leads everyone into a vacant room. Addressing Page, he says. "You've always been perceived as an honest, upstanding citizen, contributing to the good of your community. Yet you've declined to talk about the K-25 accident when others were severely injured. Two individuals, your fellow scientists, were horribly burned. One's died."

Page flinches. His face loses color.

Blankenship steps up. "Dr. Page, why haven't you participated in any debriefing sessions about this incident?" He hesitates just a bit, but I can tell he's got something else left. "Doctor," he says, "are you a German spy?"

Page's chin has sunk down on his chest. Adeline clings to him as he lifts his head and says, "I am appalled at our clumsiness when handling a substance that could be part of one of the most powerful weapons on earth. A weapon so volatile and deadly that merely inhaling the air around it wounds or kills those who operate it."

Blankenship says, "So you've washed your hands of our evil industry at K-25, is that right?"

Wearily, Page shakes his head. "I am no Nazi. No spy. My curse is knowing we are confounded by errors. Serious, egregious errors. What we are doing will surely unleash a terrible, monstrous demon on us as well as our enemies. I need to know everything will be safe. I have no assurances now. None."

Adeline has had enough. "Don't talk anymore, Solly, not about this. Let's talk about something else."

Blankenship rises. "Sergeant Chatwood, I have enough for now. I will speak with the Doctor again before he's moved to a more secure setting. No one meets with Dr. Page without my expressed approval. Sturgis only."

"I'm tired now," Page says. "The pestilence at K-25 haunts me." Adeline hugs him tight , kissing his cheek over and over. I'm not sure she heard his words.

Sergeant Chatwood steps up. "This way, Dr. Page."

We make our way past the nurse's station halfway down the hall. Then through a Sick Ward. Nurses unconcerned with us. We reach another secure area, heavy doors, wire mesh embedded in the window glass. Bars across the windows, too. Other than myself there are five MP's answering to Chatwood. They remove his cuffs, and Page is required to strip down to his skivvies. His chest, pale and slender, nearly concave. His clothes are taken away as he dons gray trousers and undershirt. He looks diminished. Somber. Helpless.

Yawning again, he takes a seat on a couch, slipping off his shoes. He leans back, reclining as much as possible, closing his eyes. Adeline sits next to him, picking up his feet to place them in her lap, settling in, massaging his feet. Moments later Page sits up straight. "I am over tired. I do not think I can sleep." He offers us a weak smile and slowly closes his eyes anyway. Keyed up, but exhausted. Or determined, but miserable.

I try to read Adeline's eyes and her expression as she glances at the MP's, evidently unhappy they're witnessing all this. Things have changed, and I'm not sure where we're headed. I wouldn't be surprised if Page jumped out the window and killed himself. I've got to do something to help.

Addie twists her brother's feet ever so slightly so he opens his eyes. "You need to do your part, Solly." She's not fussing really, somehow maternal in her tone, not little sister.

Her brother blinks twice, as if clearing his head, and says, "There are demons among us committing terrible acts. Devastating the entire world. Murdering the innocent as well as the guilty. All mankind." He whispers urgently, "Is that what you want, sister? The end of the world?"

She stares at him, murmuring words I can't understand, and his chin lowers onto his chest once again. After a moment he rises and moves across the room to stare through the barred window, which gives me a start and then some relief. He can't break through the bars. I move next to her.

"Adeline, it's going to be all right," I tell her. "He doesn't want terrible things to happen, that's all. We all want that, right?"

But as she looks back at me it comes clear I don't have the real say-so here. This is her drama. It's clear, right there in her eyes. I reach for her hands to warm them, but they're not getting any warmer. Not that I can tell. She remains fixed on her brother at the window. Solomon Page's story makes my head hurt. I can't do anything to help him. Or her. An air of sadness fills the room, and I can't see how we're going to pay for this whole situation we've gotten ourselves into. Then she looks to me, her expression blank at first, but gradually warming up, like she wants me with her. Wants me to help. To do something for Page.

It comes to me out of the blue. Something I remember that makes sense and feels right. In her eyes I see a better man than I'd been moments before. Wistfully, she smiles like she already knows what I'm going to do.

"Adeline," I say. "Tell me more about Stan Musial. Will you please?" Page turns with interest, the weight of the world shifted off his shoulders. This won't last long, but somehow it helps just now.

The Scribe

The doctor was short of breath and wheezing, but what concerned him most was the swelling at his face and neck. He was taking antihistamines and steroids, but still felt pretty bad. Worse than he had expected. He often told his patients, "Your job is to be quiet and let the medicine do its work." Easier said than done.

Over the years Dr. Samuel Friedkin had for the most part avoided illness, which, in his particular line of work, was remarkable. Practicing medicine during wartime in 1942 in a burgeoning metropolis like this Federal Reservation known as the Clinton Engineer Works could wear anybody down. This part of East Tennessee was something of a secret, playing a highly confidential role in developing weapons to use against the Germans and Japanese. The CEW was growing exponentially, and men were having construction-related accidents or they were getting sick, or they were worn to a frazzle by demanding work. Or they were drunks brawling and carousing, chasing loose women. The hospital saw it all. And dealt with it all.

Being on call after normal working hours was the true bane of his work. If he had calls before midnight and again during the earliest morning hours two or three nights running, he would be operating on a substantial deficit. That unlucky pattern had caught up with him, and that's how the penicillin was able to lay him low. From what had befallen to him he had learned he was allergic to the stuff that normally cured everyone else.

During bed rest he wished he could somehow be of more help to his wife, Linda, caring for their children. Linda did just about everything for the kids because he was usually gone to the hospital or another house call. He felt guilty because he saw all Linda's efforts, her devotion to him and the children. Her incredible determination.

The Friedkin family had outgrown their two-bedroom tract house in the Federal Reservation, and they'd built a larger home on five acres two miles outside town on the eastern side of Solway Bridge. They needed space for the six of them, husband, wife, and their children: Sammy, aged ten, Denny, eight, Pete, seven, and their little girl, Reba, who was four.

Sam was affable and easy-going, but Linda ran a tight ship with high expectations and strict routines to get the place into shape and keep the children in line.

She drove to and from school in the station wagon and gave each boy a chore according to his age and competence---collecting eggs from the henhouse, watering the pigs, hauling bottles and cans to the far side of the barn. Reba was mother's little helper all day long as Linda cleaned house, did laundry, and tended the garden. Reba was a bright, curious little female whose only blemish was her crossed eyes.

The child's condition, strabismus, prevented her from tracking an object with both eyes at the same time. She was a healthy, happy little girl, but when Linda read nursery rhymes, the child couldn't follow the words like the boys had done. She told Sam, "Each child is different. Let's give her time. Maybe she'll grow out of it."

But she didn't.

As he lay in his sick bed Sam dwelt on the rigors of his routine: he could come home from the hospital one or two days for lunch, and he and Linda would take a half-hour nap, letting him recharge his batteries while giving her some opportunity to share her thoughts. The kids were not to interrupt their brief afternoon interludes. Sam didn't say much except to answer questions she put to him.

Linda's was a succinct agenda of what was going on with each child. Lists of what she needed help with around the farm. Repairs that were needed. Plans to finish the basement so they could move the boys downstairs. She'd ask his opinion, unwilling to accept a perfunctory, "Whatever you think best, darling." He had to take a stand that proved he'd been listening. Whenever he gave her a thoughtful reply, she'd say, "All right then. I'll get that going. Now kiss me so I can rest with you a while." They would doze until he had to go back to the hospital. He put in long hours there, and Dr. Hollister, chief of staff, appointed Sam as lead physician for the new wing where Negro patients were seen. A building called the Annex. Of course, he still rounded at the hospital. That's where most of the work was.

On the second day of his recuperation her topic was Reba. "I've talked with the ocular therapist, Miss Benson, about Reba's eye exercises."

He recalled Sylvia Benson whose office was in downtown Knoxville.

Linda went on, "Reba's doing all right, but Benson's not seen much change yet. She uses the stereoscope to measure how Reba pulls one side of the page to the other, and . . ." Here she hesitated.

"And what?" Sam said. "Can she do it?"

"Sometimes. Not always."

Linda was quiet a while. He wondered if he'd missed something. Finally, he said, "What is it? Is there something else?" This effort to speak up took the wind out of his sails, but he was determined to pursue it.

She lay at his shoulder, her head resting on his arm. "I've timed the trip to Benson's office. Takes 35 minutes. I want to ask Benson to see Reba three times a week instead of just once. That will give them more time using the bar separator. But it'll cost more."

"We can handle the cost," he said.

"Well, I thought I could show Reba more about how reading works. I can write things out for her, let her touch the pencil when I make the letters. Then maybe she can try it. Maybe that way it will sink in for her."

Sam was fully awake now. "How'd you come up with this idea?"

"My sister Kate taught me my letters just like that. I was nearly seven before I knew the whole alphabet. I want better for Reba." He could hear the energy in her voice, feel it as she craned around to see his face.

He said, "Benson knows what to do. Have you talked to her about this? About changing the schedule?"

"I just thought of it this morning." She nestled closer, molding her hip against his, and he thought he'd asked the right question. They needed more information before making changes. They dozed together, and Sam didn't wake when Linda got up, sleeping soundly until supper time, something he'd never done before. As they ate supper he realized a big part of his feeling so poorly was due to exhaustion.

He'd tried to please everyone, especially Hollister and pushed himself too hard too long.

On the third day his wheezing was better, but the swelling had moved to his lips and tongue. He had difficulty drinking, spilling water down his front. Linda brought him a straw, and that worked better. His energy level was improved, and he thought he was getting a little better. He needed to get back to work. Hollister made it clear he needed him as soon as possible. He'd phoned Linda several times and was aware of Sam's progress. Reba brought him a get-well card she had drawn and colored for him. He recognized her renditions of the house, the barn, some creatures that he guessed correctly were chickens. A large, lopsided, bright yellow sun shone down on a tree, green leaves in abundance and another strange creature high in the branches.

"What's this?" he asked, pointing to the unknown creature, relieved his tongue was cooperating, no longer spastic.

"It's me, Daddy," she said.

"You?" he said. "What's this part? This square thing?"

"My rhyme book," she said. "Momma reads to me, and I know them pretty good. Sometimes I stay in my room. Sometimes I go to the climbing tree. But I can only climb up two branches. I read up in the climbing tree."

Sam smiled. "Why don't you go get your book and read some rhymes to me?"

She scampered out the bedroom door, returning moments later with a large hardback book titled *Dear Mother Goose,* which Sam had used at bedtime with the boys. She clambered over him to lie next to him, her head nestling onto his shoulder in just the same way Linda did. Sam breezed through *London Bridge is falling down, Jack and Jill, Three Blind Mice* and more, using his finger to mark each word as he read it.

Linda appeared at the door, stopping to watch their progress, her face attentive. Sam didn't know if she was more interested in her daughter or her husband. So he and his finger continued reading with Reba, *I'm a little teapot, Baa, baa, black sheep,* and *Old McDonald.* They laughed heartily at the "E-I-E-I-O" chorus as Sam touched each letter. Reba was full-throated with enthusiasm, and he was feeling better, not quite ready to go back to work, but relieved that he was leaving the doldrums. Probably back to the old grind soon.

Reba sat up, saw Linda, and said, "Momma, come see me read with Daddy."

Linda came around to her side of the bed, so close that Reba ended up on top of them both, squirming, happy as she could be. Before he could turn the page Linda brought her hand up to the chorus of Old McDonald. "What does this say, Reba?' she said, running her own finger under the E-I-E-I-O.

Reba chirped out the beginning of "Old McDonald had a farm . . ." And Linda stopped her.

"No, this part right here." She ran her fingers under the letters. There were no visual cues to aid the girl. Just the letters themselves.

Reba hesitated, looked at each parent in turn. "Horse?" she said, merrily, but uncertain.

"Try again, darling. Go on. You can do it."

Reba didn't plead for help. "Duck? Chicken?"

Linda said, "Try one last time. If you don't get it, we'll help you. Go ahead now." She rubbed her daughter's back and smiled again.

"Pig?"

Sam kissed her forehead, adding, "It's the E-I-E-I-O part." He touched the letters. "This is E. Then this is I. At the end is O."

Reba grabbed his finger and said, "I know the letters, Daddy. Let's do it again. I want to see it close as I can." Her smile was more businesslike now. If he began at the beginning, she got it right. If he mixed it up, she was wrong as often as correct. But willing to try and try again.

Linda eventually said, "Daddy needs his rest. Come help me string beans in the kitchen, all right?" And the two of them rolled out of bed, headed for the kitchen, leaving Sam to do his own debating about his youngest child's future.

On the fourth day he was able to get out of bed, although he didn't want much breakfast. A biscuit and a cup of coffee. Linda took the boys to school, leaving him and Reba. He watered the pigs for Denny and dumped cans for Pete, Reba accompanying him everywhere. When they got back to the house, she said, "Daddy, I want to read in my tree."

"Show me," he said.

She took him to a maple by the driveway, climbing up two well-worn branches where she could put her back against the trunk, her feet against at a crook in a thick branch. She recited each page appropriate to its illustration, turning to get his reaction. She didn't need a finger to follow.

"You're a smart girl, Reba Elizabeth. There's a lot of things you'll be learning in the years to come. Momma and I will help you all we can, but Miss Benson's going to help you more than we will. You do as she says, all right?"

Reba nodded.

"Do you like her?" he said.

"She's a good teacher. Funny, too."

At naptime Linda nestled onto his shoulder and said, "Benson has agreed to do three visits a week. If

Benson can't help Reba learn to read, we'll have to go another way. I'll have to do her reading for her. Her writing too." Linda sat up, looking back at him. "I'll have to be at school with her," she said. "I can drive all four kids to Elm Grove Elementary School and just stay with Reba. I know it's not such a big school, but I'm friends with the principal. Clarence Jordan is nice as he can be. I think he'd let me help her. I could sit next to her and read for her, write for her. I'd have to be quiet, not bothering other children. Reba wouldn't need me for arithmetic. She's smart as a whip. Can count all the way to a hundred already. The problem is reading. That's what I can do for her. And, of course, we'd need to get some help around the house."

She was dead set on it, not really asking him if she should do it. Telling him what she had decided. It was out of the question, of course, but he wasn't ready to tell her that.

"Have you spoken to Benson about this?"

"We talked about how Reba tends to skip from one line to the next, omitting nearly half a sentence. She's not able to read a line and find the next line on the page. She skips lines."

"You've just sprung this on me. I need to think how it would affect the boys. I mean, is it fair to them?"

Color rushed into her face. "I think it could just . . .Well, no, I haven't figured out how it would work for everybody. That's true enough. But if she doesn't learn to read on her own, our little girl's going to need help."

She was dealing with worst case. Not interested in wishful thinking.

He said, "But what if she gets better, gets to where she can read like her brothers?" Which was how he saw everything playing out if Benson was as good as advertised.

"Reba might just do better than her brothers," Linda said, and her voice had that little show of flint which persuaded him that he ought not push her on this. Not now. Linda was absolutely resolute in her intent to compensate for strabismus, to find some way to overcome it. She was that way about nurturing her boys, too, but there were three brothers and only one sister. So Reba was her mother's alter ego, precious beyond estimation. Cherished in an extraordinary way that three boys could never equal. He needed to think hard. There was more to this than reading.

Linda said, "I don't want to cheat the boys or Reba's teachers. Or you. What I'm talking about doing . . . I'll give it my all. You know that."

"I do," he said. "You follow through on things."

"I try to," she said, sidling over next to him, her chin nudging his arm, which he rearranged so her head was back on his shoulder. "All right," she said, lifting her face to his. "Then I need you to kiss me."

He did, and she settled back down. "You're better. I can tell. No swelling any more. You'll go back to work tomorrow. But you need to tell me what you think about Reba and me before you get too busy at the hospital. Hollister wouldn't be sympathetic. Sam was amazed he hadn't already been summoned back to work. You'll get distracted by all your patients. You'll take care of everyone else but us."

"I know," he said. Certainly, he'd be swamped. That awareness kept him from napping. He was already gearing up to fulfill his Hippocratic oath at the hospital or the clinic. Linda had the primary oath here at home. He marveled at her resolve, her grit and pluck.

He shut his eyes to relax, but could not dispel visions of rows of student desks filled with first graders. Way in the back of the classroom sat Reba with Linda nearly adjacent in a larger desk, whispering to their daughter about Dick and Jane. Linda would write down Reba's every answer, praying with every fiber of her being that school would allow them this privilege for as long as it might be needed.

Which might be always.

Bitter Comfort

Time had come unsprung somehow for Loretta Chastain, who at twenty-seven was just as pretty as she'd been in high school. That's what Red always told her, but here and now she felt uncertain about a few things, such as exactly how long had she'd been away from him. She'd left her husband and his buddy, Arvin, at a table in a dark, smoky corner of a place called the Dew Drop Inn. Rhonda Scurlock was there, too; she was Arvin's date. And there was this other guy named Buckley. She didn't even know his first name. Just Buckley.

A petite brunette, Loretta felt slightly woozy and unsteady on her feet. People, mostly men, were staring. That was okay. She caught every male's eye in the place. She did it at McCrory's Department Store over in the Federal Reservation called the Clinton Engineer Works. She was a cashier and knew she was eye candy, but what of it? She was counting on it. Her face wasn't really outstanding, except for her large, brown eyes, which Red likened to the moon shining in a dark pool. She liked it when he talked like that.

Loretta had drunk too much too fast and would readily admit, if anyone asked her, that, "Yeah, I'm drunk. But what of it?" Taking a deep breath she stood, beer in hand, surveying the dim surroundings near the door to the Ladies.' She urgently needed to pee, but wanted to finish this beer first. Should have had something to eat. Peanuts at least. She was lightheaded, and the air in the lounge was humid, heavy with mingled scents of beer spilled on the floor and strong cleanser to disguise it. The owner of this place, Fagan was his name, he ought not have the stinking Mens' and Ladies' so damn close to one another. A person might just puke.

Wiping moisture off her upper lip, she wondered if it would be better to step outside a little while. How long had she been gone from Red? Couldn't remember. This much she knew---late October, 1944, just west of Knoxville. A tavern on Highway 25W. Just yards from the Anderson County line. She was damned sure the air was better outside than in this close funk, getting jostled, bumping into all these bodies coming and going to pee in the dark. All the tables and drinking, cussing and fussing. Juke box way too loud.

She thought how Red, who was older than her, thirty-one years old, could've been twin brother to Arvin, always laughing the way they did. Like fools.

She really needed to pee. When she got ready to go back, she wasn't sure where she had left off. She had been momentarily content to be lost inside the Dew Drop's Ladies, withstanding the odor, at least for a while. But now she started moving back into the big room, and the next thing she knew she was tableside again.

As she was sitting down, Red was talking, although she couldn't hear much of what he was saying. Probably still complaining about his job, plumbing for Roane-Anderson. He was always right on the edge of quitting or getting his ass fired. His face was splotchy again, light shining on him so you could see that irregular blemish that always came up on his neck when he was drinking, which was pretty constant. His nose looked like he'd got sunburned since arriving at the tavern. His hair had that flying away look like burnished wheat in a stiff breeze. Him and his long, horsey face, taller than all the rest so you could see him pretty good. Red, the center of attention.

"Buckley," Red said, "Tell us again. What was it Betty did in court? What did she say?"

Buckley ran his hand through his slicked back hair and took a long pull from his beer. Loretta thought Buckley's hair was darker than it ought to be because Buckley was older than all the rest of them. Fifty? Fifty-five? Maybe older. Skinny and wiry. No beer belly like Arvin. The little guy whose sharp weasely eyes could creep you out if you looked straight at him, if he happened to be looking straight back at you. Loretta didn't know where he was working now. Buckley moved around a lot.

Watching Arvin's face, Loretta couldn't help but see him as a round-faced little boy with his pudgy fingers, and there was his body odor. She wanted to tell him, "Go to the Laundromat, for Christ's sake. Wash your damn clothes!"

But she didn't. Wouldn't do any good, so she didn't bother. He'd worked overtime all that Saturday and had come late to the Dew Drop to spend his hard-earned pay. Lost some out behind the building playing dice, but figured he'd earn some back betting against Buckley. Of course, that didn't work out for Arvin.

She thought Buckley was a funny little guy. Not funny ha ha. Funny peculiar. He had done a lot of crazy shit, but none of those details came to mind just now. Being as the War was still on, Buckley was serious as a heart attack. If he was backing something…say, a bet of some kind or other…it wasn't smart to bet against him.

"Well," Buckley said, "Betty was brought up to court wearing them orange overalls, you know?"

Loretta looked again across the room at Fagan's waitress, Betty Pemberton, her so tall, pale, and slender. Betty took her time with her tasks, never hurrying to get through. It was like she actually enjoyed wiping down tables and waiting those same tables amongst drunks and soon to become drunks. Most of them common laborers working for J. A. Jones building dormitories and barracks for the Army. People were coming in every day and night to get jobs. It was tough in some of the jobs, but the pay was really good.

For several months now Buckley and Betty had been going hot and heavy, even though she probably wasn't half his age. Red had said something about them doing "Something vertical out in the parking lot a few weeks back." Loretta could guess easy enough what that meant. Red had his impatient acrobatic side, too. And acrobatics could be interesting or sometime better than just interesting. She tried to visualize tall, skinny Betty coupling with scrawny, little Buckley. Couldn't see it though. Couldn't picture it.

Loretta thought Arvin Ledbetter was closer to marrying Rhonda Scurlock than Buckley was to marrying Betty Pemberton. It wasn't so much what the guys did as it was how they did it. It was how the guy treated his woman. She thought about this kind of stuff more and more these days, and she usually ended up remembering how she'd stopped playing cards with Red. They used to play a lot of Rook, and she won time after time, and that pissed him off. She felt sorry for him eventually and purposely let him win a game. She said, "Wow. You really got me that time." Leaning across the table to give him a congratulatory kiss, expecting they might just get vertical acrobatic right there on the floor. But Red didn't even pucker up, letting her lips embrace his sullen mouth, scowling at her. "You gave me that trick. You done it on purpose. Don't do that again."

"Why?"

"Because, if I take a trick, it's mine. If you give it to me, it ain't really mine. I don't like it when you do me that way."

That turned the milk of her generosity into sour clabber, and she sulked while he sulked, and they didn't get romantic for two weeks and sure as hell not acrobatic. The whole damn thing got out of hand altogether. It showed how a man could screw up things with a loving wife. Proved her point. Good old fashioned respect was in short supply.

Loretta glimpsed Betty as she listened to Buckley's story about her on the witness stand. Betty could overhear while she worked back by the jukebox.

He said, "Then Judge Shoopman asked her, 'So exactly how did this play out, Miss Pemberton? I see here you claim he had relations with you when you were under the influence. Both of you had been drinking for several hours. He wanted to be intimate. You refused. He grabbed you, and, as you put it, overwhelmed you and had his way with you, standing up against a pick-up truck. Is that about it?"

Red giggled, chugging away at his beer, as did Arvin. Red egged Buckley on. " Tell it. Tell the whole thing."

"'Yes, Your Honor, she says, and Shoopman ast the big question, saying, 'Well, Miss Pemberton, how do you explain that Mr. Buckley, who is several inches shorter than you, was able to consummate anything with you standing up like that? He couldn't exactly reach you, could he?'

"'Well, Your Honor', she says. 'I had to hunker down a bit.'

"Judge slammed down his gavel, hollering, 'Next case! Next case!'

Arvin loved all this, hollering, "Next case! You hear that, Red? Next case!"

Buckley swigged his beer, watching all their faces, satisfied at the telling, but with a twinge of boredom, as if he didn't need to tell it all again.

Betty's face turned beet red, and she walked quickly past two tables and out the back door. She was the only waitress working, so it was going to get interesting in a hurry if she didn't get back. Loretta wondered, *Is she angry? Ought to be.*

Red turned to Loretta. "How'd you like that, Lo?"

"Not so much," she muttered. "Rhonda don't either, do you, Rhonda?"

"I don't have no opinion one way or t'other," Rhonda said. Then she burped quietly, placing a finger to her lips. Loretta didn't know how many beers Rhonda'd already had, but, of course, it was too many. Rhonda was only twenty, working at a plant called K-25. She never talked about her work. "I can't say. The boss has let go four other girls for talking too much. I need the job, so that's that. I'll not say a word, you hear?"

Arvin thought so too. "You're drunk."

"So're you," Rhonda said. Her answer, slurred and surly.

"So are we all, I reckon," said Red. "All of us, buzzed, right? None of this is gonna see the light of day anyhow. It don't mean shit. None of this stuff."

"How do you mean?" Arvin said.

Red took a pull from his beer, studying Loretta's face as he did it. For a brief instant she was proud of him for taking charge. Her Red was a good man most of the time. Had found them a home in one of the J. A. Jones trailers only about a mile from Solway Gate. Red brought home a fairly regular paycheck. And usually wasn't hard to make up with when they disagreed, though they seemed to be disagreeing more these last few months. And spending more time at the Dew Drop, too. Not just weekends, but sometimes Tuesdays or Wednesday nights as well. Spending money with nothing to show for it. Nothing to speak of.

"So, Rhonda," Red said. "You really don't have no thoughts on Betty's hunkering?"

Rhonda stayed silent. And Loretta took bitter comfort in being right about these people around her. Impaired and reckless with one another. Mean as snakes, liable to pile on you if they saw you scared or fragile. It was a downright free for all. But they're good folks when they haven't overdone it with alcohol.

Loretta didn't much care for Arvin any more. And Red was getting to be a selfish prick, a lot like Arvin. But they needed to be drinking to keep a truce all night long, and sometimes drinking just made things worse. If Arvin had trouble with Rhonda, he could just take her home and then head back to his place. They were more or less living together at her apartment, but, if they had a fight, he could slink back to his grungy little trailer up in Bear Valley to let things blow over.

Red didn't have a trailer to hole up in. When Loretta fought with him, he'd act pissy around their place. He'd be like that a day or two. Or else he wouldn't come home at all, carousing with Arvin at the Dew Drop all weekend long. Sometimes he'd drive over to a club in Clinton or Harriman, but more often than not he'd head to Grove Center. That was what she didn't care for, not one damn bit. His constant carousing. And she was also tired of Buckley's making fun at Betty's expense. And she'd had it up to here with Red's crap.

Another waitress showed up, a fat woman, probably sixty years old, with cotton candy hair, limping and bringing with her a smell like old cheese or maybe something overripe in the kitchen. She grabbed a cleaning rag, jumping right in on wiping tables. Her name was Dorothea.

"You go on, gal," she said. "Take yourself a little break. I got this."

Betty did more collecting empties before heading out back, and Loretta decided she was sick to death of cigarette smoke and beer and darkness where there should have been light. There was only the red neon Schlitz sign behind the bar. The rest was dark blue velvet with a few orange dots glowing, cigarettes showing through the smoke.

Loretta headed to the Ladies again. Around the second corner she banged slam into Betty who was coming in the rear door. She wore no make-up. None. Her auburn hair pulled back in a short ponytail. Plain as day, ill at ease, nervous as a cat.

"Catching a breath of fresh air?" Loretta said.

"Uh, yeah," Betty said. "Actually, I just looked at the airplane store for a while. I always do that."

"Airplane?"

"Yeah. Over there. Past the gas station."

Loretta had a vague recollection. The airplane thing, whatever it was, was closed down after dark, not lit up, so she didn't really didn't know much about it. Never paid much attention.

"Show me," she said. "I want to see this airplane thing."

They went through the gravel parking lot. Traffic whizzing through the long curve of Highway 25W headed east into Knoxville. The light from the Texaco station was just sufficient to make out one of those gimmick ideas, a building in the form of an airplane. Sort of a boxy looking thing with wings high up on the side like it had landed right next to the highway, and you could drive up, park, and walk under the wing right into the front door of the place. At one time it had been a gas station, but now it was more like a shop or flea market, trinkets and knickknacks in its windows. Cheap stuff.

Betty cleared her throat. "Sometimes I have this dream that I'm flying to a wonderful place. A calm and quiet place. A farm with a creek close to the house. In my dream I jump slowly up into the sky, floating like a cloud. Steering myself isn't easy, but I push myself up over houses and trees. Up away from...."

Suddenly she was silent.

Loretta frowned, "Don't leave it there. It's interesting."

Betty finally said, "Sometimes I need to get away from the tavern, all that loud talk and meanness. I got this cousin down in Georgia. Cousin Karen. Her husband Ted and her, they live on a three hundred acre farm near LaFayette, not far from Chattanooga. Up in the hill country. They call it Duck Creek Farm."

"Huh?"

"That's the place where they camp out. Duck Creek runs through bottom land. They got an old shack probably eighty-five to ninety years old sitting about two hundred yards from the road. Plus two barns. A truck. A tractor."

"Uh huh."

"Ted's building their cabin high up on the ridge."

"Thought you said they got a shack."

"Oh, they do," Betty said. "Ted's a carpenter, and he's always talked about a cabin on a mountain somewhere. They got a steep eastern ridge, and he's building up high so you can see down the creek. It's peaceful at Duck Creek, not like the bars, certainly not like the Dew Drop. Not like the CEW with all the dust and mud and smoke and lights, the traffic and noise. All the commotion is just too much, you know?"

Betty went on about this Duck Creek place while Loretta listened to every word., wishing she had thought to bring another cigarette or beer. Or a sweater. It was cooling off rapidly. She folded her arms across her chest and realized she didn't really want the beer. It would be best to sober up and find some peace and quiet like Duck Creek Farm. She couldn't remember a time when she turned down a few hours at the Dew Drop. It was like a long-standing habit for her. She wondered, *Is that a good thing?*

Time unsprung from itself again, and Loretta drifted in and out, catching occasional snippets of what Betty was saying. "Whippoorwills down by the creek. Turkeys grazing through the hayfield…and deer you can feed corn to around dusk every evening, if you've a mind to."

Betty's voice was so genuine and sincere. The place Betty was describing, it wasn't sounding that different from the twenty-three acres Loretta's daddy had owned on Black Oak Ridge over in Anderson County. Where Loretta had grown up was in the valley-and-ridge country west of the Smokies. Windrock Mountain just a little south and west, and the small crossroad communities of Dossett, Marlow, and Frost Bottom in the lowland between the ridges.

Suddenly, Loretta shivered uncontrollably, not from cold, but from memories rushing back around her. Memories of the night calls made by barred owls her Daddy always said were like dogs barking in the dark woods. Glowing eyes of raccoons raiding their backyard, illuminated by a young girl's flashlight beam. Sunset burnishing clouds burnt orange and gray over the Cumberland Plateau. And on a cold autumn morning fog surrounding the barn and sheds with silhouettes of fawns and does feasting on spilled corn nubbins. All this forgotten for so long, now come back to her, distinct and sharp in memory. So different from the Dew Drop scene.

There were kitchen smells when Momma cooked breakfast. Eggs over easy. Grits. Bacon. Sausage. Best of all, large misshapen buttermilk biscuits. Loretta used to beg for a dollop of raw dough, licking the tasty lumps off her fingertips. Momma didn't allow it, but, if Momma was otherwise occupied and Daddy was tending stove, he'd whisper, "Bunny, come here. Get you a biscuit to sop up this bacon grease.'"

Daddy long gone now, as was Momma. Loretta would give anything to hear him call her Bunny again. Give even more to smell his familiar male scent that spoke of cigars and time spent in the barn or field where he had sweated and toiled every day of the world. She remembered his big arms around her when she was real little sitting on his lap. Sometimes she sat in his lap in church. Back in the days when she went to church.

She felt a sharp pang of regret at how she'd drifted away from him and Momma, too, when she had started filling out on top. And she'd drifted away by doing all manner of things with boys Momma'd said were too old for her. She didn't listen and started staying out too late. Started smoking. Drinking. French kissing. Longing to be touched underneath her clothing.

Touching boys right back. Sometimes coming home long after her parents had gone to bed, occasionally without the underclothes she'd been wearing when she left the house. She'd left her Daddy and Momma long before she actually started living somewhere else. Before she got too good for the country and moved to town and all the drinking places, all the gambling, the sleeping with guys she hardly knew. Had just met.

All this was something else from a long, long time ago.

Now she'd got a pretty fair glimpse of the world Betty Pemberton was talking about. A place and also a time she was surprised to be yearning for. She thought it might be all right, different from what she'd thought she wanted. But she wanted it. That was for sure a surprise. She wouldn't have told anybody, wouldn't have said it out loud. But there it was. Right there for her to think about.

She murmured, "If wishes was horses, beggars would ride."

Betty didn't understand. "I probably told too much about Duck Creek."

"Well, I used to live on a farm that sounds like Duck Creek. It sounds awful nice," Loretta said.

"It is to me," Betty said, "just like it is for Karen and Ted."

"Tell me about Karen."

Betty said, "She's just pure gold, you know? She's pretty as a picture, tall like me. Her Momma and mine were cousins. I used to spend summers down there. I druther milk cows, slop pigs, and tend the bantie hens than keep on doing what I'm doing now, but I ain't got no choice in the matter. Everybody's drawn to the CEW because the pay's so good. Doesn't matter what it's really for."

Loretta hugged herself tighter. Partly due to the chill outside, but also due to realizing her life was no longer simple and wholesome. It had slid ever so gradually in the opposite direction. Loretta Chastain had changed too much. She wasn't sure what she'd become. Wasn't sure about much of anything.

Betty said, "You ready to go back inside?"

She told herself, *Wish I could just fly out of this whole shitty situation with Red.*

Inside the back door it was warm and loud again. Everything much too close and dark.

Betty sensed discomfort. "What's wrong?"

"I don't want to be here any more. Don't like these people. I can see you don't like them either, and you got much more reason than I do. How do you stand them?"

"Oh, I don't know," Betty said. "I hope people will be nice. Not laugh at me. After that business in court, I'm just tired of all of it."

"I won't tease you," Loretta said. "Won't let others do it either."

Betty looked skeptical, "Red will do what you say?"

"If he knows what's good for him," Loretta said. "Sometimes I have to straighten him out a little."

And she thought, *That is, if he don't beat the crap out of me first.*

She loved him. She did. But, swear to God, he just couldn't behave himself, and sometimes he was quick to smack or choke her, so she had to give as good as she took to hold him off. Once she'd used a metal folding chair on him when he was drunk on his ass. Mean drunk he was. Even so, it had been a good thing for her he'd been in the hammock when she hit him, or he might have hurt her bad. She kept swinging the chair like a hammer, catching him smart on his head and shoulder. Stunned him right proper, but he was starting to get up, and she knew if he set his feet solid, it might not go so good for her. So she kept on flailing away at him with him yelling and cussing her, and her screaming right back at him, neither one understanding the other. While the metal cut him a couple times, and he started bleeding like a stuck pig, he wasn't really hurt.

She had run into the house, locked the windows and doors, found the cleaver in the knife drawer, and sat down with it a little too fast, plump, right on the floor by the fridge, stunned, waiting for him to try to get in. It wasn't long before he was banging on the doors and the side of the house. If she needed to, she'd cut him if he got in, but eventually he just stopped cold where he was and drove away. She thought, *Must have lost his key*. She stayed awake all night in the dark, wondering if he'd bust in on her. She double latched the front door. Stacked pots and pans inside the back door where the lock was suspect, so, if he came at her that direction, at least she'd hear him in advance. She felt better with the cleaver close by. The phone rang a bit. She let it go.

Next day she skipped work at McCrory's, holing up in the kitchen all day sitting on the yellow linoleum. That afternoon when the phone rang again, it scared her. She didn't answer. Twenty minutes later when there was a knock at the door, she peeked out a window to discover it was Rhonda, not Red.

Later sitting at the kitchen table, Rhonda asked, "What happened?"

Loretta explained, and Rhonda said, "I knew it wasn't what he told Arvin."

"What was that?"

"He said some guys tried to run him off the road outside Oliver Springs, and he stopped and took em all on. Beat the shit out of em, but they got him a little bit, too. When you didn't answer your phone, I thought it didn't sound right. So here I am."

"Is he all right?"

"Cut ear and lip. Bruised neck. Otherwise fine." Rhonda lit a cigarette. "Why'd you all start fighting anyway?"

"I caught him in a lie about a little blonde bitch working at Queener's Florist over in Clinton. I told him she'd be the last one he'd ever cheat with."

"What'd he say to that?"

"He just swung a little in the hammock like he hadn't heard. So I said, 'Red, I might just cut you off, if you get my drift. Stop giving you any.'"

"And?"

"He said, 'Maybe you will. Maybe you won't.' And he spit at me. That's what he did, but he missed me, but not by much. That's when I tore into him with the folding chair. Oh, Rhonda, if I'd had this cleaver, I'd have cut him." She opened her purse so her friend could see it.

"You don't mean that!"

"The hell I don't," she said, but she wasn't so sure now how she felt about Red. She had spoken about what she felt before. Talking about the hell of not having a man she could trust, a man who was used to beating on his woman, hearing herself so bitter that it took her aback. She was ashamed of what she was feeling now, but, by god, she sure was feeling it.

Rhonda was still there when Red finally did come home, sober as a trial judge and dirty as a mud wrestler after a full work day. To their surprise, he unlocked the door without so much as howdy do. "Hey, girls," he said, walking past them toward the bathroom. Soon they heard him showering, and Rhonda whispered, "He won't try nothing while I'm here."

He'd shaved when he came out, dressed in fresh jeans and one of his dark blue work shirts, smelling of Vitalis and soap and mouthwash. When he sat down at the table to smoke, Loretta saw he was tired and over their upset, even though his lip was swollen and split. No animosity in his eye. Calmed all the way down. Or else forgot the fracas.

Loretta thought, *We're all right.*

That time she turned out to be one hundred percent correct.

Back at the Dew Drop all this about the beatdown with a metal folding chair came back to Loretta as she walked through the crowded room back to the table where Arvin and Rhonda sat with Red. When he saw her coming, before she got within earshot, Red put his hand up to his mouth, hiding something he was saying, which made Arvin laugh. Rhonda sat stone faced.

"Hey, Loretta," Red said in a simpering, too sweet tone. "Where you been, Baby?"

"Get me another beer," she told him without looking his way, knowing he didn't like it when she ordered him around. But off he went without comment.

When he brought her a Budweiser, she chugged half right off, without engaging in the conversation, and Red gave her plenty of room, not challenging her sulk. This part gave her a dread feeling that she and Red were headed to a bad end. But she had no idea how to go any other way with him.

There was no logic to it because he was unusually polite, making a show of trying to be nice. She couldn't explain it, not even to herself, but the anger and spite was deep set in her marrow. That night she was trying to drink it away, but the feeling just settled in like the flu. Later, looking back on it, she saw that was when things had soured for her and Red.

She learned more about Betty when she was off duty one night and ended up partying with them. Buckley introduced Betty to the beer-and-a-bump thing, and they were all laughing and hollering, "Go, Betty, go!" She tried another beer, looking like she was caught by surprise by the whole thing, so much so that she tossed her cookies right outside the door to the Ladies.

Later she confessed to Loretta that this was like before, a couple years back when she'd been too damn crazy. No. Worse than that. Open to going with anybody who paid attention. Sleeping with guy after guy. A lot of guys. "I lost jobs at Lewallyn-Millers, at Magnet Mills, and Clinton Drugs. Got lucky with waitressing here at the Dew Drop. I thought I hit bottom a while back, but now I don't know. At least I ain't on probation no more. Not in jail again. I'm trying to stay outta there, if I can. Stay out of trouble. Find a man to hang onto. A good man."

"Uh huh," Loretta said, unsure if Betty was thinking Buckley was the right answer.

She spent a lot of time considering Red that way. He was the one that mattered. Loretta started watching him like a hawk. Watching everything he did. She knew doing that, paying that much attention, was going to jinx things for them because she knew Red Chastain better than anybody else in the whole wide world. He was fair to middling, but not really as good a man as she deserved. He was tall and good looking, and he was always in the middle of things, laughing and joking, but she couldn't trust him any farther than she could throw him.

Drinking helped her think about other things, but it didn't change anything really. Not for long. Her Daddy always told her, "Bunny, remember this---The leopard can't change his spots."

Red's spots were all too clear.

She didn't know what was going to happen with him, but she didn't feel good about things. At the same time, she didn't know what else to do. So she didn't do anything, and they just kept on spending most of their money night after night, drawn to that old high life at the Dew Drop.

But she kept the heavy blade in her purse. It just barely fit. She felt stupid about carrying it around, but at the same time she counted on having it to counter the jinx she knew was following them. Would follow them even unto the end. When Arvin went to jail for stealing from a shop at Grove Center, Loretta thought that could possibly undo the jinx somehow. Maybe with Arvin gone, Red would change for the better. Become worthy of her trust.

Apparently, the boss at Grove Center Shops, Mr. Chapman, had been watching Arvin for months. He was going back after hours and had liberated an item or two here and there. Pieces of silver, too. And jewelry. He got sentenced to six years at Brushy Mountain State Penitentiary over in Petros.

So Loretta was keen to see how Red was going to react to Arvin's getting thrown under the jail. Anyone else would see the same old-same old Red carousing at the Dew Drop, but she saw some tiny chinks in his armor. He was subdued in a way she'd never seen him, and she felt he wasn't caring as much as he used to. *But he really misses Arvin,* she told herself. *He's not going to move on. Not going to forget his old buddy.*

But what really got under her skin was he shunned Rhonda. He didn't say much to her and her date, Ricky, when they came to the table. He wouldn't stay seated when Rhonda was sitting there. So naturally Loretta took up for her friend, spending more and more time with Rhonda while Red sat at the bar chewing the fat with Fagan. Or sat on the other side of the room with truck drivers he knew. Or he'd take up with outright strangers, be they male or female.

"Who's that?" Rhonda said, nodding at a buxom blonde Red had found.

"Don't know her," Loretta said.

They sat watching awhile and being watched by those who knew them and knew why Arvin was gone. Eyes were bouncing from Loretta to Red's new girl and back again. Blondie allowed Red's arm to stay around her shoulder, which got Loretta sniffing impatient and huffy. While she was watching, Red slid his hand a little lower.

Rhonda said, "You got some itch needs scratching bout this new gal?"

"Yeah, well…" Loretta said.

"Why's Red running from me all the time?" Rhonda said, blurting it out suddenly. "I ain't done a damn thing to him. Arvin's the one that screwed up, not me."

Ricky chimed in with, "Might not be you. He don't even know me. Maybe it's me."

"No telling," Loretta mumbled. Then she stood up so quickly she got lightheaded, leaning in Red's direction, putting her hand on the table to keep her balance. Then she came back, grabbed her purse, and headed for Red again.

Walking around the table past the jukebox, time slowed down again just a couple of seconds as she approached Red. He turned just as she got close enough to say something, but it was Red's hand moving on Blondie's thigh that caught Loretta's eye.

"Red Chastain," Loretta said, "this girl with you, her you've got your hand wrist deep in her lap…Do you even know her name?"

Obviously embarrassed, the girl looked away while Red stared back at his wife. He took a swig from his beer to buy some time. Loretta had her purse like a shield out in front of her. It was a long moment just like that. Like a photograph you took and framed for a wall in your kitchen. Frozen forever.

His throat blemish darkened as he swallowed. "Don't believe I do know this gal." And he was grinning. He put a hand on Loretta's hip and shoved her back so rough she fell against an empty chair.

He didn't see what she yanked out of her bag. She was quick with it, flailing away at him, catching his knee, hip, and chest, wailing like a cat as she hit him, slashing back and forth again and again. He was jumping back sideways, scrambling to get away, hollering all through it, "No! No, nooooo!" When he was clear, and she had stumbled, falling to her knees. he put his hand on his midsection where she'd sliced him, blood seeping through his fingers.

Betty was there pulling Loretta's hands off the blade. Fagan hovered over Red where he'd slid down on the floor. Nobody else was coming close.

Fagan told Red, "Just hold on, buddy."

Blood started pouring out of Red's pantleg running out at the cuff. She must have hit an artery. His eyes wandering, catching Loretta's, almost too late. All he said was, "I'm cold, Loretta. Cold."

He bled out in about three minutes, his face losing nearly all its color. The blemish on his neck disappeared altogether in that brief interval, which would be the last of his life.

Betty had the cleaver. Loretta was slumped on the floor, moaning hoarsely. No actual words. Just misery. She started up loud again when she saw blood on Betty's hand.

"You got me, too," Betty said. "Just here on my knuckles. I'm all right, I think."

Now Loretta let out a screeching howl, so agonized and frightful that most of the place cleared out. Fagan ran his customers out. Not Rhonda and Ricky. Not Betty. Tears still streaking down Loretta's face.

Later, she remembered very little of what happened that night at the Dew Drop. She wanted Betty to come see her after they put her away, she knew that much. When the judge pronounced her guilty of manslaughter, she got thirteen years, and the time she spent in the Anderson County jail waiting for transfer to Brushy Mountain State Penitentiary was quiet and calm. She was the only female in the place for six days and nights, and she had a lot of time to think things over and settle into damnation.

When she got to the prison, she wanted Rhonda to come visit her, too, and Rhonda would be the one to come most often, usually twice a month, but when Betty came, those were the best visits. Those days were what Loretta lived for.

Time was changeable, but prison was always hard. Loretta was never unsteady on her feet, never woozie, but her time was sprung all to hell most of every day and even more at night. Of course, there was no liquor, and she had trouble sleeping most nights. She had some trouble with other inmates, got roughed up a couple times, and was skittish about talking with anybody for a few weeks. She didn't trust the fat girl who was in the cell with her. Her name was Becka, and she was big-boned, but soft all over with serious acne scars, and she had more time ahead of her in prison than Loretta---seven years more. Some nights Loretta woke to hear quiet sobbing from Becka's bunk. Loretta tried to talk to her, but such opportunities inevitably turned out to be tearful affairs, focusing completely on Becka who couldn't hold an idea about anybody else in her head for more than an instant.

Loretta got assigned to the laundry where she did ironing. She burned her fingers a few times, so they took her off that kind of work altogether, and she was left in her cell with her hands bandaged. While she healed on the outside, she was changing inside, too, probing for things that should matter.

When her hands were well, she got her hair cut short, and she lost the taste for most prison food. She wasn't so pretty now, and she started avoiding mirrors. She was quick to do as she was told. Many's the time when Rhonda would be looking back at her, face up against the glass in the Visiting Room, and Loretta would ask, "When's Betty coming back?"

Loretta could see the hurt in Rhonda's eyes the instant it came out of her mouth. And every time Loretta reached out to her, explaining, "I'll always love you for coming to see me, Rhonda. I'm beholden to you and always will be. I *want* you to come, Rhonda, but I *need* Betty to come." In times like these Rhonda would choke up, tears welling in her eyes, nose running. Trying to smile. Unable to speak. Just nodding. Backing away from the glass.

Rhonda gave way so Betty could take a seat at the glass next time. Betty said, "I can share time with Rhonda, if you want."

"No," Loretta would answer. "Let's just visit, the two of us." Loretta would prompt her with questions. "What was it like building the cabin up on the ridge? Did Karen ever tell you about that?"

"Well, yes," Betty said, playing with her hair down by her collar. "Karen said they would drive up from Atlanta on week-ends in Ted's truck with the camper top. And they'd work on the cabin and camp out with sleeping bags every night. They brung a Coleman stove for cooking meals. They had rented that old shack out to a family that worked the fields for them. Karen's a second grade teacher. Did I tell you that?"

Loretta said, "So you mean like sharecroppers?"

"I don't really know how it worked," Betty said. "You're asking stuff I don't know how to answer."

"Okay, don't get flustered. How'd they clear the spot on the ridge for the cabin?"

Their allotted visiting time was half what Loretta wanted it to be, and Betty was directed to depart, saying, "I don't know if I can answer much more about Duck Creek for you."

Loretta saw her flush and looking down at her feet as she backed away from the glass.

"Don't go, Betty!" But she said it too loud, and her face must have been too anxious, too fierce with the need to know because Betty flinched, eyes wide,

117

looking back at her, but leaving fairly quick. Quicker than usual.

Betty didn't come back when Loretta hoped she would, and she asked Rhonda about it. "Have you seen her? Why ain't she come back?"

Rhonda said, "I don't know. She ain't at the Dew Drop any more."

"Where'd she go?"

Rhonda hunched her shoulders. "Search me. Maybe J.A. Jones or K-25, that new plant."

And it wasn't a week after that that the administrators at Brushy Mountain changed the visiting regulations, restricting visitors to no more than one visit per month, and even then visits were limited to twenty minutes apiece. So Loretta lost track of Betty and Duck Creek Farm, and then Rhonda missed a few visits herself. She explained once because of a flat tire. Another time she was sick.

So Loretta was on her own for a good long time. She turned inward, not saying much to anyone else, not causing trouble, just looking at herself as close as she had ever done. Solitude clothed her like a well-worn garment worn threadbare.

She lost track of how long she'd been at Brushy Mountain, and the sadness lasted so long that most of the hurt went away. She forgave Red a hundred times and wished she could take it all back and have him around again, even as little as she trusted him, as jealous as she was with all those blonde temptations he kept running into, as shitty as it had all turned out there at the end. She even wished for old Arvin again, wondering if he might be there at Brushy Mountain, too, on the men's side.

One day she was wrestling with some wet sheets in the laundry when the supervisor said, "Chastain, you got a visitor."

"Me?"

"You get twenty minutes."

She dropped everything and hurried down the hall, her heart beating like a jackrabbit's. When she got through the last door and into the Visitors Area, there was only one chair left on her side. Four cubicles were occupied with women intent on talking with their men. She hesitated because there was just the one chair, so she must be supposed to sit there. The other side in front of her was empty.

She sat down before she noticed a tall, slender woman standing by the exit door on the other side. The woman seemed shy and hesitant, but, when Loretta sat down, this woman sat across from her, smiling kindly.

"I'm Karen Wood," she said. "Betty Pemberton's cousin. I'm awful sorry. I should have written you a letter or something to introduce myself. Tell you I was coming"

"Don't apologize," Loretta said. "I'm just so…I got a million questions for you. That's all. Happy to be meeting you. You got no idea how happy I am."

Karen's cheeks flooding with color.

"Tell me about the farm," Loretta said. "Please tell me."

"I will," Karen said, "but first, if you don't mind, tell me why it's so special for you. You've never even seen the place. You don't know me."

Loretta said, "I grew up on a place like Duck Creek. And Betty told me about your place. So I got curious about you and Ted. Never thought I'd meet you though."

"That was Ted's doing, I guess. His and Buckley's."

Loretta reached up to the glass. "You know Buckley?"

"Sure do," Karen said. "He's out in the parking lot with Ted. They're big buddies."

"He's a character, ain't he?" Loretta asked.

"Never met anyone else like him," Karen said. "Unless it's my Ted."

They laughed, and Karen put her palm up on the glass. Loretta put hers there, too. Palm to palm. It was like they were old friends somehow. Loretta wasn't sure why she felt like she did.

They sat back, and Karen talked about how Ted was all into the details making Duck Creek a good place to live. A place they could leave Georgia for.

Karen said. "One time Ted told me, 'I know how you are about taking baths and washing dishes, so I reckon we need to have reliable water.' That's how we got our well."

"And one week-end he said, 'Wouldn't it be nice to have a one-room cabin here instead of hauling bedrolls and the Coleman up here every time we come? We could have a place to leave our gear.' We did the framing and flooring ourselves, but we had to get somebody else to do foundation work."

They talked as fast as they could, especially whenever anyone else would get up and leave the room. Karen told about the calves they had. "One heifer had twins, and you know that, when that happens, one usually gets rejected."

"Yes," Loretta said, recalling how Daddy had dealt with those situations. "One time I committed to bottle feeding an orphan two quarts twice a day. The heifer liked to killed it. We had to tie up her back leg and put her in a headgate, but she was just too cantankerous even confined that way, so I took over."

"We had twenty-five calves this spring," Karen said, "and all the others bonded well. But this little white-face baby was so young, she didn't even know how to suck. She wouldn't go for the nipple on the bottle, and I didn't know what else to do. Ted said, 'Pour some of that milk on your thumb, and stick it in the little gal's mouth and see what happens that way.'

"Well, I did like he said, and she went to town on my finger. Didn't notice when I pushed the nipple into her mouth and slid my finger out. She was starved."

"Time's up," the supervisor said, and they had to quit too soon.

She smiled as she stood up, adding, "Glad to meet you, Loretta Chastain."

"Will you come back?"

"Sure, I will," she said, and Loretta was pretty sure that would happen. She owed Betty for getting with Karen, persuading her to visit one of her friends in jail. Later, she would wish she'd asked about Betty. Should have done that.

That night Loretta found some portion of true comfort, a taste she almost didn't recognize. Bittersweet it was. She had a calm, restful night's sleep. Next morning she recalled a dream. Like Betty, she recognized the lay of the land she flew over---over Windrock Mountain down into Frost Bottom, and over the gravel road that led to the homeplace, and there was

Daddy waving at her, walking behind a mule, plowing down toward their creek. It was pristine. All good like it had been when she was a little girl. Back when she was good.

It was a wonderful dream that came back often, never getting old. A dream that left her feeling a little better every morning. That dream carried her through the rest of her time at Petros, and when she was released two years early for good behavior, she knew what kind of place to look for. Where she could start over.

If You Don't Know the Words

It took me half a year to stop singing the song Walter Lancaster tried to teach me. That's how I saw what he was trying to do. That's what I called it--- singing a song. His was a melody that told a story about getting corn, tomatoes, and beans growing fast and tall. I listened to him singing it, but I found out the hard way his melody was sinister. I still don't know if his fertilizer was poison or venom or some kind of curse. All I know is it was real, and it was brand new, and it laid me low. There's still times now and then when I get addled, and I misremember the simplest things. I'll see something in my mind's eye, but can't keep all the details straight. That surely came from that infernal fertilizer which tainted my corn, and it is surely Walter's fault. Maybe mine, too, because I chose to trust him like that. Even so, if I'm patient, some clarity will come back to me. But you know I can see some things pretty clear, like the day Walter first sang that

125

damned tune for me. At first I believed he was a righteous singer, but I was terrible mistaken.

At my front door he stood, hat in hand. "Hidy, ma'am. Are you the Miz Delap I see writ on the mailbox?"

I said, "That's me---Ida Rose Delap."

He said, "My name's Walter Lancaster, and I'm here to share an amazing new fertilizer with you, if you're interested." His Adam's apple stuck out on his neck, and his voice broke a couple times as he spoke. "I been working at Stooksbury's Farm over in Oliver Springs. That's where we're testing the new stuff. But, you know, things don't always go as planned. As I was driving thisaway this last bottle of the stuff which I must of missed somehow, it rolled out from under my seat. And, well, I didn't want to turn around and head back to Stooksbury's. And I sure wasn't going to throw it away." He gave me a shy grin. "Would it be all right if I spread this last bottle on your garden? I seen you got a truck garden out back. I got more than enough fertilizer here. And I can check back with you in a month or so." He was one of those fast talkers. I was looking him over, noticing things about him and couldn't help but see he had ants in his pants, wanting to get back to the War Effort at the Clinton Engineer Works.

"All right, Walter. If you'll answer my questions about this stuff so I can get some idea of what in tarnation it is, I just might let you do it." He picked up the bottle, waving it around so we could see the stuff swirling around. It was coarse, black sand, sort of greasy and shiny to boot. Like nothing I'd ever seen.

Leaning in confidentially, he said, "The big Army bosses don't know everything. They're having us wear special gloves when we handle this stuff. Weighing what we start with, then what we've got after we're done. They've brought in inspectors to watch us every single minute now, but me and my buddies already got what we wanted. We just needed to find somebody interested in improving his yield. We were lucky to hook up a week ago with Stooksbury. I mean, we ain't partial to price freezes and ration books and all the new regulations coming down on top of us. We're determined to make a buck our own way, not the Army's way. If this stuff works like we hope it will, we'll make a fistful of money, but I ain't charging you a cent today. Not one red cent."

The Office of Price Administration was causing a lot of trouble for farmers and merchants all through 1943 and now into 1944, so I could see Walter's point, plain as day, his initiative, his private enterprise. Finally, he said, "Do we have a deal? Can I sprinkle some of this stuff around here and come back and see how it's all going? Is that all right with you?"

I said it was. And looking back on it, that was fateful. He wasn't a bad person, and I don't give him all the blame for what happened. I should have known better my own self. Walter's fertilizer turned out to be devilish cruel. I got poisoned after eating vegetables he fertilized. Without knowing it, I got took. If it hadn't been for Dr. Stauffenberg, I'd have been a goner. I didn't have money to pay doctors and nurses that take care of me. I couldn't pay off the Clinton Engineer Works hospital for the five weeks I was there. Every night when I was trying to get to sleep I didn't have good prospects for tomorrow. I was pitiful: sick in body, mind, and soul. But by and by I woke up realizing I wasn't going to be snake bit much longer. I still felt pretty awful, but I was turning the corner, and that was enough to hope for. You can stand just about anything if you got hope.

It helped that Stauffenberg took care of the bills. He was boss of the Army scientists in the CEW, and he came to my room that very first day while I was nauseous, that bitterness lingering in my mouth. He said, "We were lax handling things on our end. So we'll not have you paying for our mistakes. If you'd allow us some of your tissue samples, blood samples, and the like for future study, we'd appreciate it immensely. We'll cover your expenses no matter what your answer might be. We'll look after you, Mrs. Delap. You have my word." He was looking me straight in the eye when he said it. Laying it out straightforward for me. Fair and square. If I'd help him out, he'd take care of me. So that's what we did. Helped each other out.

I never would have believed I could have lived through what happened in 1943. Or what's took place during the War since then. Everything everywhere's going fast. We get news from all over the world. Like General Patton getting blessed out by Ike for leaving the Russians out of the glory party when we finally defeat Japan and Germany. They's still furious fighting in the South Pacific and Europe, but things are mostly looking better.

I don't dwell much on the news. I set right where I'm at, watching these Woodson children running around in their Daddy's grocery. Tilde has hired me to watch her brood three or four days a week, which is real work, let me tell you. Thinking about the kids, I glance in a window where my reflection reveals an old woman's face, crow's feet wrinkles around her eyes, long gray hair tumbling out from under her wide-brimmed straw hat. Someone that looks more tired than I feel. Someone who's got trouble keeping up with young 'uns.

Their Momma, Tilde, ends up taking Toby, who's just turned four, and Kathleen, aged six and a half, inside for supper. I'm about ready to leave the grocery, but Earl meets me at the door. Tilde must have heard him coming in. She yells to him from the rear of the store, back where the family lives. "Earl, if you can hear me, pick up the phone. Rabb says he's got news."

Earl Woodson picks up the phone by the cash register, and hearing it was Police Captain Rabb brings me to a full stop. I need to know the news. Earl doesn't seem to mind I'm right there with him. He's on the phone only a couple of minutes. When he hangs up, he reaches for a pencil on the counter, scribbling something, tearing off the scrap of paper, stuffing it into a pocket. He stares at me, muttering, "1371."

"I beg your pardon."

"Oh," he says, blinking at me. "Hello, Ida Rose."

"Hello, Earl. What's this 1371? Is it important?"

"That's Charlie Rabb's phone number. He said to call him if we see a dark Ford pickup truck with New Jersey license plates." He takes the paper out of his pocket, glances at it. Puts it back.

"Who's driving a dark Ford pick-up?" I say. "Crooks?"

"Could be. Charlie says this could be a black market situation. Somebody's stealing ration books, then stealing rationed items. Selling false ration books. Causing all kinds of trouble. Charlie's not sure what's going on. He's calling them suspects. Not just for the damage they done here, but also for one of the barn fires last week."

"So you had something stolen?" I say.

"They took my big auger, the one I use digging postholes. And my socket wrenches. That hurts more than losing the auger. I use those wrenches nearly every day."

I say, "Do we know what they look like?"

"Nope. Rabb gets all the law enforcement people communicating about thefts. Reports get sent out. He says it could be two or three men using that truck. He's put out an APB on them."

"A what?"

"'All points bulletin.' He's got all the law enforcement in CEW looking for that truck. Keeps the Anderson County people up to speed. Knox County sheriff, too. I can't figure out why they hit us like they did. They just ruined some food that anybody might purchase. Didn't take much but a few bags of sugar and my tools. I get some of my produce from over in Solway, and they hit us over there, too. Maybe it's somebody with a grudge against me."

"I've never heard anybody bad mouthing Earl Woodson."

Tilde hollers again. "Earl, we got to take the kids to church. You need to change your clothes."

"Coming, I'm coming." Earl moves toward the front. "Let me walk you out. I got to lock up." We make our way down the aisle. "How're you getting home?" he asks.

"Walking."

He stops abruptly. "That's no good. I'll get Ronnie to take you in the truck."

"Oh, that'll be too much trouble."

"You'd be doing him a favor. He's hellbent to drive something every day. Tore up a tiller on my John Deere last week. Banged the station wagon's rear bumper yesterday. That boy wants to drive everywhere, whether it's tractor or truck. Tilde and I will be taking the station wagon into Clinton, and he's got to take our pick-up to get a load of produce at Kramer's over in Solway. Then he can take you home. If you'll wait out front, Ronnie'll be along directly."

Soon I'm listening to the family depart, the sound of their vehicle fading as it heads east. Ronnie comes in, unhurried, smiling, and relaxed because he's not under Daddy's thumb just now. He's a big boned teenager with a mop of blond hair that needs cutting, freckles on his nose, his clear blue eyes studying me. He's built like his Daddy, but his face resembles Tilde more, especially around the mouth. Come to think of it, he favors Walter Lancaster a bit, too. He gives me a blank look for a moment, and then says, "I guess I need the truck keys. I'll be right back." He rushes out the way he's just come in, returning shortly, rummaging around the cash register, hunting the key. Finally, he says, "Here we go," waving the key, beckoning me to exit with him right through the front door.

Once he gets going, he's not a bad driver, but getting started is herky-jerky, full of hiccups while he's in first gear. He's okay in second and third, but there's plenty of stop signs, and it takes us nearly twenty minutes to get from Elza Gate and cross through the Solway Gate. Twice as long as should of.

It's after six o'clock by the time he's unloaded his empty crates at Elmer Kramer's In-and-Out Store. Elmer's one of those bald-headed fellows who's trying to hide his shiny scalp, which draws your eye when he'd like you not to study him too close. Bald men are funny that way. Elmer's in a hurry to get home for supper, so he says, "Pull the back door shut when you're done. When you hear a click, the door's locked good and proper." With that, he hurries out to his Buick.

Ronnie exchanges empty crates for similar crates full of cabbage and okra, and he's about done when I glimpse movement as a vehicle rounds the corner of the store, puzzling me because the store's closed. *Maybe Elmer's come back for something.* Besides, the vehicle isn't headed for the loading dock. *Why would anybody park back behind the building?* Ronnie looks puzzled, too.

"Did you see that?" he says.

I nod, feeling kindly blind inside the In-and-Out while there's such mysterious goings on outside.

Suddenly serious and cautious, he says, "I'm going to go look."

"What kind of truck was it? What color?"

"Not sure," he says. "Black or maybe dark blue."

I move closer to him, lowering my voice. "See that little window, the high one on that wall? Can you get up on that counter there and look out first? I'd feel better if we knew more about who just got here. Wouldn't you?"

"I would," he says, his eyes flickering to the window. Putting two hands on the counter, he vaults up onto it with surprising agility. He peers through the window, immediately hunching back down so as to avoid being seen.

"There's two men getting out of a dark Ford pickup," he whispers. "One's carrying a crowbar. They're headed around back."

"What about the other fella? He got anything?"

"You want I should take another look?"

"Try not to let them see you."

He says, "Maybe we should just wait a while." So we listen quietly, and we hear some noise from out back. A thumping noise, three loud knocks in a row. Then a sharp cracking sound like something's broken. There's voices outside, but no more noise. No more knocking.

He creeps up to the window again, popping up quickly, looking both directions, and then comes off the counter to stand next to me. "They're back thataway," he whispers, pointing to the rear of the store. "Back by the store room doors."

"We got to stop them, Ronnie. They're up to no good. And driving a dark truck. Did you see the license plate? Is it a Tennessee plate?"

"Didn't look for that," he says, and he vaults back onto the counter before I can stop him. He looks and jumps back down. "Not a Tennessee plate. Not sure which state it is."

We're staring at each other. "If they're breaking in, they don't want anyone to see them do it," I say. "They'll probably run like Snider's pup if we come up on them." I let that sink in. Not sure that's a good idea, but it's already been said.

"I'm going to go out the front door and walk around that way," I tell him, pointing toward the highway. "They won't hurt a old woman." I'm listening to what I just said, hoping that's right. The part about not hurting a old woman.

I'm trying to handle all this so Ronnie won't do something rash. Don't want him to make trouble for us if we can avoid it. When I hold my hand out to look at it, it's shaky. Ronnie notices my tremble, and I wish he hadn't seen it. I try to steady it, but I'm not successful, so I quit trying. I just let it fall to my side. That engine around the corner's still idling.

I don't wait for Ronnie to change his mind. Taking a deep breath, I let the screen door bang as I head out the front door. I got no idea what I'm going to do if I come up on somebody in the truck. I just put one foot in front of the other again and again. That's all I can manage, all I can come up with in the moment. So I'm walking along slowly, wondering what Ronnie's doing. I should have told him to be still.

Suddenly, I'm hearing footsteps, someone running around the corner, and in the same instant there's an automobile engine revving up, getting louder. Then a second engine cranks up. It's happening fast, and I move to get a good look at that license plate. When I turn the corner, Ronnie's truck has run slam into the building and into the other truck, a dark blue Ford. There's Ronnie sitting behind his steering wheel, his hands gripping it tight, white-knuckled as if he's got plans to push on through that wall and the other truck. His engine revs up too loud with gray smoke billowing out the exhaust pipe, tires jerking a quarter turn, slipping so the truck hasn't moved yet, jammed hard against the Ford, angled against the wall. I'm not sure the vehicles can pull back from one another even though the Ford's engine has quit. The fenders are crushed together. Locked up tight.

What's he doing? Why's he...?

There! I see a face grimacing through the Ford's windshield. A stranger's face right there behind the steering wheel. Ronnie's trapped him. He's staring at the fellow, and I'm not happy with what I see in Ronnie's face. *He's done this on purpose.*

"Stop it!" the man in the Ford yells. "Back up, you little shit! Back up!"

Ronnie guns his motor, but without letting the truck move forward. The man in the Ford screams in terror. When he runs out of air, it's clear nobody's going anywhere.

Wasn't there another man? I ask myself.

"Ronnie, what happened? What did this guy do?" The truck Ronnie's driving eases back a couple inches, which is a good sign. Ronnie's face has changed some. I know him now. He's listening to me.

"You said stop them," he says. "This was all I could think of." He turns his attention back again to the Ford, peering out his windshield. "I'm not sure how long I can keep this up."

"I'll call Charlie Rabb," I tell him. "Do the best you can." I turn to go, then turn back. "Where's the other fellow? I don't see him."

"He's there," Ronnie says, nodding at the wall.

"What?"

I step back a few steps, leaning down to peer under the chassis. The second guy's right there, partly obscured by the front left tire. Can't really make him out. The breeze shifts, pushing a cloud of exhaust fumes over him so you can't hardly see him. I look to Ronnie, "Hold on. I'll be right back."

Rabb answers at 1371, and I say, "Charlie, this is Ida Rose here at Kramer's In-and-Out over in Solway. You need to get somebody over here. We got two men here. Might be the ones who ruined Woodson's corn. They could be your barn burners. They're here. Both hurt."

"Okay, okay," he says. "We're coming."

Back outside nothing's changed except the man behind the steering wheel has slumped down a little bit, and Ronnie appears awful tired and a bit scared, too. I can see it in his face. I take my place by the truck, trying to get a better look at the man under the chassis.

By and by, we hear a siren coming our way, and finally, a police car pulls in behind Ronnie's Chevrolet in a cloud of dust, and Charlie Rabb gets out. Three uniformed officers pile out of the car. Like always, Charlie's chewing on his unlit cigar. He's a wiry fellow, not so tall as me. He comes over to us and says, "What's the story here? Who's this fellow?"

I let Ronnie explain. He's kind of pitiful, stuttering, searching for the right words, "He's…I mean, they…I saw them, and…and…."

So I step in. "That's all right, Ronnie. Let me tell it." The look on his face touches my tender side so much I want to haul him out of the truck and hug him tight, but instead I say, "I think we got them." And I tell Charlie how all this took place.

Afterward, Charlie says, "Turn it off, son." And he points his officers to deploy on either side of the truck. Once the engine's off, Charlie approaches the man pinned behind the steering wheel and says, "How're you doing, buddy?"

"I'm hurt bad," the fellow says with more energy than I thought possible. "I'm hurting, I tell you, and I'm going to sue this boy for running me down. My partner will sue him, too. We…."

"Save it," Charlie says. "Let's take this one thing at a time. What's your name? I know this boy and the woman. I don't know you."

"I'm Paul Jenkins," he says, still surly, glaring at Ronnie. "From Orange, New Jersey."

I can't help asking, "Is this your truck?"

"No, it's my partner's," Jenkins says. "What of it?"

"Where's your partner?" Charlie says.

Jenkins scowls. "Some police you are! You don't even know he's right under the truck. This boy's the one that hit us. Not the other way around. He's the one responsible."

Charlie squats down so he can see under Ronnie's vehicle. Standing back up, he tells Ronnie, "Best get out of your vehicle, son. We need to back off so we can assess damage."

One of the officers had bent down on the other side of the truck, and he stands back up and says, "We need an ambulance."

Charlie opens the driver side door. "Get out, son. We'll take it from here."

The officer on the other side of the truck says, "Sir, there's something else here. Might be what we've been looking for."

Charlie turns to me. "Where's that phone you used to call me? I don't want this call to go out over my car radio."

"Inside the store," I say. "I can show you." I get Ronnie by the arm. "Come with us, Ronnie. After Captain Rabb makes his call, he'll want to hear your side of the story." I glance at Charlie. "Is that how it needs to go?"

Charlie nods. "We still got to sort everything out. I saw some equipment in the bed of that Ford that's got Woodson writ on it. Might have been stolen from Earl. It was half hidden by tarps. I pulled them away, and there they was. Jenkins here claims Ronnie tried to run them down for no reason. Somebody could be going to jail."

I can't read Charlie's face as he says all this. Ronnie's eyes widen, and he goes pale. Then paler.

"Let's go back inside," I say. And Ronnie follows along like a young pup.

Half an hour later the ambulance is here, and they're loading up Jenkins and the other man. Charlie's been on the phone three times, and I think he's got things under control. He takes me aside to get my version of what's happened. Then he does likewise with Ronnie. Then he goes back through it with both of us together. When finished, he tells what's going to happen next.

"Alvin Treadaway's the fellow stuck under the truck. He's touch and go. Jenkins has most likely broke a leg and a few ribs. He'll be okay, I think. Not sure about Treadaway." Charlie turns to speak to Ronnie, and I get the feeling something important's coming now. It's not important for me, but for Ronnie, and I don't want him getting in trouble because of these two men. Jackasses from New Jersey. That probably ain't kind to put it that way, but that's how I feel.

Now Charlie's looking at Ronnie again. He asks, "The tires slid in the gravel. Did you say that? You were using the brakes, but the tires slipped in the gravel, right?"

I see a place to jump in. "Charlie, I can vouch for Ronnie here. Shoot! He was just doing what I told him to do. Doing it best way he knew how."

Charlie says, "I know that, Mrs. Delap." He turns to Ronnie. "You're going to be all right, buddy. But we got to do everything by the numbers. I believe what we've been hunting's in Jenkins' truck. Now those egg head fellows, those scientists will be happy to get it back. But they'll ask you a jillion questions about it, too. Don't take all that personal, Mrs. Delap. Just tell them everything you know, and let them do what they do, even if it don't make sense."

Charlie pats Ronnie on the shoulder, smiling at him, "You did good, son. Just tell the truth, and you'll be fine." It's like Charlie's his uncle or older cousin, trying to make Ronnie feel better, but is Ronnie buying it? He's got a great stone face. Charlie walks away, speaking to one of the uniformed officers. Abruptly, he returns, his face suddenly serious. "Neither one of you touched the things in the Ford, did you? I mean in the truck bed. None of that, right?"

"No, we didn't," I tell him.

"They're going to test you. Don't take it personal. The new things they're working on in the plants, the ones they're making, they're…I don't know what they are. Nobody does. Nobody knows what the new stuff might do to you."

This rings true with me. I can remember last year and my sickness after the business with Walter Lancaster and ultimately with Stauffenberg. All of it so long, long ago. Nobody knows what's coming tomorrow, so we got to be ready for whatever comes. Keep the faith. Keep trying. Keep singing the tune even if you don't have the words.

Soon Charlie Rabb's turned us loose and driven away, leaving his men tending the trucks. Ronnie's quiet, and I'm watching him for signs about how he's handling all this rigmarole. We've just coming out of a whirlwind, sort of winded, trying to catch our breath. He surprises me, saying, "I better get in touch with Momma and Daddy. They need to know what's happened. Especially Daddy." His face seems older than his years.

"Right," I say. "We should have done that already. I can talk to them, if you need me to."

"That's a good idea," he says.

We do some plundering for the In-and-Out phone book so we can first call Elmer. Give him a head's up. He's none too happy about what I tell him, hanging up before I've said goodbye. He's coming right back. Ought to be here in six or seven minutes, tops.

Nobody answers at Memorial Methodist in Clinton, so we wait a minute and try again. Still no answer. Ronnie glances at the wall clock. "They might still be eating downstairs. That's what happens first on Wednesday nights. The kitchen phone doesn't always ring down there." So we keep on waiting.

I make the next call, and I let it ring and ring. By and by, a female answers, "Hello."

"This is Ida Rose Delap," I say, waving Ronnie to come to the phone. "I'm here with Ronnie Woodson. The boy needs to speak with his parents. Can you get them to the phone?"

"Sure," she says. "This is Dorothy Lewis. I just saw Mrs. Woodson. I'll run get her. There's nothing wrong is there?"

I say, "We had a situation earlier. Everything's fine now. Ronnie wants to let them know." I hand him the phone. "They'll get your Momma."

He holds on a while, finally talking to Tilde. Listening to Ronnie's remarks, I can guess how Tilde's soothing him, listening to what he's telling her. The talk with Earl might not go the same way. After he hangs up, before he even turns around, the phone rings.

"Go ahead, answer it," I say. Ronnie blushes as he picks up, and he listens a moment before giving me a look that indicates he wants me to take the call. "It's Mr. Rabb."

"Hello, Charlie," I say. "What do you need?"

"Ida Rose," he says, and then he hesitates, which chills my heart. *What's going on? What's happened?* But I keep my questions to myself, holding my breath. "Ida Rose, that Treadaway fellow is dead. Keep Ronnie right where he's at."

The rest of our conversation slips right past my ears. I answer back to Charlie, but I'm unhappy with how he sounds. He's not so friendly as before. He's official, and all the while Ronnie's staring at me I'm not sure what to tell him.

The addling washes back over me, so I set myself down in a cane-bottom chair, reaching out to touch Ronnie. I begin seeing something that might show the way to go. The thing to do for Ronnie. It leaves me feeling exactly right, answering everything, but I can't see details yet. Just this marvelous something taking shape before me.

Ronnie's staring down at me, looking confused and upset. "Miz Delap, are you all right? You doing okay?" He squats down in front of me. Eye level. Sweet, sweet boy.

I nod to give him an answer, patting his hand to get him to wait a bit. I'm peering through a kind of fog to see a familiar face forming in front of me. Someone I think I know. *Is it Walter Lancaster?* I ask myself. *Who might this be?*

I think to open my ears a bit. My eyes, too. I see him now. See him in my mind's eye.

Stauffenberg.

I keep listening, too, waiting on the righteous words to come to me. Let them come on not like some magical promise. No, no. Instead, let them come on like a hymn.

First, Do No Harm

By March, 1945, Helen Jones had got herself a job as a hospital maid. She was the first Negro maid hired there.

Back home, which was some three miles outside Gadsden, Alabama, the Jones family had been doing without for two long years, just barely scraping by. There wasn't even enough money for shoes for her baby brother. That's what hurt Helen the most. It was hard times for them out in the fields. Too dry, sun burning up whatever it was they put into the ground. Not nearly enough rain to yield proper crops. Everybody, including the children, working every day, even after church. Not to dispute against the holy day, but to find any little advantage when they could. It was desperate hardscrabble.

On one fateful Sunday Helen's Pap decided to do something unthinkable: he was going to spend eight dollars for Helen to catch a bus up to East Tennessee, because he'd heard a place called the CEW, not far from Knoxville, was paying the best salaries he'd ever heard of. Herself, she had all of a dollar forty cents to see her through. That was all he could sparc. Pap gave her a long, tender hug and said, "Go find out, daughter, about this thing called CEW. If it works out for you, help us homefolks, if you can." What Helen thought he really meant was *Find out if Coloreds can get a job up there, and watch out for yourself.* Pap was gambling she could do both.

Getting sent away hurt deep, but she knew it would be one less Jones mouth for him and Nan to feed, right? It would leave only seven Joneses on the farm, her sisters and brothers, all of them younger than Helen who was just about to turn twenty-two. She hugged every one of them several times, her little sisters clinging to her a long time in her lap. Her Nan wasn't much of a talker, as tired out as she always was, but she laid a hand on Helen's shoulder a good long time while they were talking about Tennessee. A good long time, but all too short.

When she got off the bus in Knoxville she was wondering where to go, trying to find some of that work. She sat on a bench figuring on things when she heard a man at the ticket windows calling out, "CEW bus leaving out of Gate 3, first come, first served." She thought that was the place, but just to be sure she went to his window. "Please, sir. Is that CEW place where the jobs are?" He said, "It sure is, but they don't take just everybody that gets off the bus. Tickets will cost twenty cents, gal." The bus was full of men with a few women. Negroes sat in the back. When they got dropped off at CEW it was hustle and bustle, traffic coming and going, and construction everywhere you looked. Smoke drifting all through the valley.

After several false starts she finally found the Employment Office and later didn't remember all the things they asked her. She volunteered for midnight shift work wherever it might be because most women, Negro or White, wouldn't touch night shift work. But Helen took to it right away, glad to have it. She would make fifty-eight cents an hour, which would be enough for her to send seven or eight dollars home twice a month if she could, leaving about twice that to live on. Living in a little square flattop house called a hutment with three other Colored girls. Didn't cost but fifty cents a week to stay there. It was the best money she'd ever made in her whole life. More than her Pap was making. She was lonely, but stayed lively on the job.

All the Negro gals in the CEW were housed in an area called The Pen, which was row after row of hutments in the Scarborough Village area. Men housed elsewhere. Hutments were just four walls and a wooden floor. Three windows cut out of the walls to give cross ventilation and a smidgen of daylight. Wooden shutters supposed to keep out the rain. No window glass, no screens on the windows. No electricity. No running water, but they brought in buckets, big buckets of water for drinking and cooking and washing clothes. Taking a bath was something you did at one of the bath houses down the row. And somebody emptied the toilet and hauled the human waste away.

Helen made a friend of Pearlie Booker, who worked the early day shift also as a hospital maid. They saw each other at shift change, and were the only Negro maids, although seven of the twenty or so orderlies were Colored. Her that was coming off shift would tell her friend about any problems that came up, doctors to steer clear of, orderlies you could count on, and them you shouldn't. When one of Helen's hutmates left a note on her cot that said, "I quit this damn place," she just disappeared, so there was no reason to wait to see who would be sent to take her bed. Helen told Pearlie, "Come on home with me. They's a bed just come open. Take it before they put somebody in it." So that's what they did. The man who came by to see if there was this vacant bed didn't make a fuss about Pearlie. He just took the gal who came with him to another hutment. Pearlie was so tickled she danced a little jig in the middle of the floor.

Helen was big-boned, dark-skinned, and built like a field hand, and so not worried about attracting unwanted male attention. She had little trouble riding the free bus from Scarborough Road to get to work a couple miles across the valley. Pearlie was light-skinned, like she was partly creole, her facial features delicate and attractive. Helen considered her a tiny, little angel. Pearlie rode daytime buses, anxious about all the men that looked her over, up and down. She told Helen their faces clearly showed what they thought of having her so close. She got the back of every bus, getting pawed and pinched, so she was all jangled up and scared whenever she was on a bus, worried about the next time she'd be on another bus. Any bus. Men weren't much interested in Helen.

At first Helen and Pearlie just happened to work on the hospital ground floor, not on second or third, so they knew all their nurses, orderlies, and doctors. When Pearlie had trouble with somebody, she explained to Helen how to get past that kind of trouble. Helen did the same for Pearlie, but didn't usually have so many problems as her friend.

Each floor had a Store Room where a lot of things were stored. Necessary things. You needed to know what was in short supply to make things stretch out to the next delivery, what soap and cleanser worked best on what sort of stain, blood, piss, or puke. Helen did better cleaning up, but Pearlie was better hiding things, wash cloths, towels, bars of soap, and what all. She put the good stuff on a low corner shelf behind a mop bucket so Helen could use it next shift, not leaving it for any White folks.

Linens were folded up and stacked, shelf on shelf. Crisp and white and clean. First time Helen went in there by herself she stayed a little while, looking it all over, smelling how purified it was. While looking around she overheard a voice: "Dr. Preston at St. Mary's in Knoxville. Get him on the line." There was more, but it faded out, muffled so she could hear the voice, but couldn't make out the words, like somebody talking inside the wall. Toward the back wall she heard the voice clearer. A male voice. White man.

Might have been Dr. Friedkin. But maybe it was Dr. Hollister, the Main Doctor. That's what Helen called him. Didn't know much about him. Didn't see him much, and he wouldn't talk to you going down the hall. She decided she was hearing both doctors, and one was talking about doing right by every patient. "We ought not give a man anything we don't know will help him. We can't just try something new and hope for the best." She didn't know what else was said because the voices started fading out to nothing. They must have left the room or wherever they were. She told herself, "I need to tell Pearlie we got to be quiet in here."

She picked up a stack of towels, bringing the soft, white fabric to her face, breathing in the sanitary scent. Antiseptic was hospital talk for clean. Dr. Friedkin used the word antiseptic all the time. He was a nice man. Didn't talk down to her like she was stupid. Now and then he had her do some things orderlies were supposed to do, but it didn't bother Helen, and she was good at jumping right in to do whatever he needed. She didn't really mind. Nearly every night he was on duty he'd ask someone to send her to him. "With you, Helen, I don't have to worry things won't get cleaned," he told her. "We got to do our best with our patients so they'll recover. Each and every one of them." Helen liked him more every time he spoke to her.

She cleaned rooms where sick people had been staying or were still staying. She mopped floors, stripped off soiled sheets, made beds up, and took dirty linens to the laundry chute. She scrubbed where men had puked or shat themselves or merely shed their blood. Some were sick as dogs; some lying there dead. White nurses and orderlies wouldn't clean up after dead men, but Helen knew doing such work would help her keep the job. And she felt the same way Friedkin did. Taking best care of every man she saw, treating them all best she could whether they were White or Colored. The Colored didn't get what Whites got, not nearly as much as the Whites, but she would keep on getting paid, and she and Pompey could get married someday. Trying to get a leg up on life. Doing better than Gadsden, that was for sure. She sent money home without knowing if it all got there. Without knowing if it was helping those who needed it.

It surprised her when Pompey Ellis got close to her. It wasn't like he was trying to get her to go to bed with him. It seemed he admired her, thought about her different than just wanting to have her. He was different than any man she'd ever known. He drove a water truck most mornings all through The Pen, and he drove a sewage truck every afternoon. That's how she first met him, when he was bringing in water. He knocked out two shifts daily, which he wasn't supposed to do, but the boss man for Septic Works couldn't find anybody else to drive the damn shit truck, so Pompey was temporary kind of permanently, making good money.

Pompey had two guys in his morning truck, Stanley What's His Name and Pompey's cousin, Zander Poteet. Stanley was medium build, always chewing a toothpick, not the hardest working guy on the crew, but Pompey liked him. Talked to him a lot. Zander was fairly puny, not much bigger than Pearlie, and he was sickly now and then, especially after visiting some of the gals in The Pen who liked to entertain visitors. Usually drinking was involved even though the MP's patrolled The Pen right often, hunting for liquor that wasn't allowed, making sure the men were gone by 10 P.M.. They ran Zander out pretty regular. Helen kept waiting for Pompey to tell her Zander was quitting, or he was going to the Hospital Annex where sick Coloreds saw the doctors. If he got put into the Annex, she wasn't sure he'd ever come back out.

Pompey was taller and thicker-built than just about anybody. Mind you, not fat. Muscles like iron such that his shirt bulged like it would rip down a seam. When he hugged her, he made Helen feel like his own little angel. Every time he kissed her, he was whispering, "You're my sweetness, Helen. That's for sure." And that's the way she felt---sweet as he could make her. Saving sweetness just for him someday.

One day Pearlie didn't take either of the first two buses to Scarborough, waiting to talk with Helen. She looked around to see if anyone was listening and said, "They's a new doctor here. Nice looking young fella. Dr. Carter, The head doctor, Hollister, brung him around today. They asked me how I was doing and who else did I know. I told them you're the best worker in the whole place. You best introduce yourself to him when you see him coming through the ward. He looks you square in the face. You watch for him, you hear."

Helen took that to heart. She'd be on the lookout for Carter, wanting to get on his good side to see if she could be his favorite like she was for Friedkin. There was new people coming in every day to work the hospital. Some going out, too, quitting or fired or whatever. Mostly, they were orderlies that were changing. They were lowest in line, then maids, then nurses, finally doctors. Helen didn't fool herself in believing she was high up there as a maid, but she thought she was one of the highest maids because she would clean up after anyone or anything. She was always busy making things new and clean again. Antiseptic.

And Pompey, he got new workers on his truck. The head man at the Water Office told him he needed to supply more hutments with morning water and come back after lunch to pick up their night soil, too. "We're giving you two new guys to help with the loading and unloading. You're still the driver, if you want, but get your crew working extra til all the hutment toilets are emptied every afternoon."

Pompey said, "These new men, where they at?"

The boss whistled up loud and shrill, and three Colored men came away from the crowd of men standing around the trucks, smoking their cigarettes. One was a tall, bony fellow, café au lait colored, who walked up first, friendly-like. "This fella's called Big Alvin, as you can see." Big Alvin shook Pompey's hand. Another man was older, dark-skinned, bad teeth, one missing on top, two on bottom. Seemed nice enough. He shook hands firm. "This is Ebb Cade. He's from North Carolina. Greensboro, right?" Ebb nodded, mouth shut, hiding his teeth. The last one was Lucas, a strong guy not so big as Pompey, but powerful legs and big hands. The boss said, "These boys been mixing concrete, but they can do whatever's needed. Boss em any way you like."

Pompey had the new men start off riding in back with the water, and Stanley and Zander rode in the cab, like always. After every stop Pompey switched them around so every man rode some in back and some in the cab. A couple of times Pompey jumped out to move the heaviest water or to help bring the sewage bails back to the truck. Big Alvin, Lucas, and Ebb did okay with the water, but not so good with the stink off the shit. They got better by end of shift, partly because Pompey wasn't too good to get in there with them handling human waste. That was the job. Pompey said,

"Fellas, all this is just good bidness That's what we get paid for." No need to complain.

Pompey was told to haul an extra 500 gallons of water to a new place just thrown up the day before, off Blair Road, but that trip turned out to be bad bidness. There was a big truck blocking one lane, jacks set up on both rear wheels. Pompey slowed down, waiting to see if there was on-coming traffic. Didn't see none, so he pulled around the truck in the road right into a dump truck going the other way, smashing into his truck head-on. The sun was rising behind Pompey's truck, and the driver must have got blinded just at the wrong time. That guy, a White man, didn't even get scratched. Only ones in Pompey's truck that got serious hurt was Zander and Ebb, who both took it bad. Zander broke his left ankle and probably broke some ribs. He was gasping and crying, unable to say anything you could understand. They lifted him out of the back end, laying him out on the ground. Then they saw to Ebb who looked to have a busted arm and both legs broken plus one broken wrist. He told them what was hurting, his voice calm and ever so quiet, but his eyes showed pain. Slowly, he used his good hand to rub his chin and told Pompey, "I got the arthritis in both knees, so some of my troubles ain't new."

Himself, Pompey was bruised some. Nothing he couldn't handle. Stanley was all right, better than the rest of them. Lucas and Big Alvin was pretty good, too, Big Alvin with just a banged up shoulder he was moving around to loosen up. Pompey looked around to see where they were. Not far from trailers and maybe a store. Pompey told Stanley, "This truck is ruint, so you need to run down to the next place that might have a phone and call the boss man. See if he can send another truck. And a doctor. If you have trouble dialing, ask them to dial for you."

By a half hour later the boss man had sent a truck that Pompey drained all his water into, and him and Big Alvin and Stanley took it to make the delivery as directed. Another truck was collecting Lucas, Ebb, and Zander to take them to the hospital. Late that afternoon when Pompey got off duty, he went to visit the men at the Annex. Dr. Friedkin, he said it would take a week to ten days to get them so they could move around with crutches. "Healing will proceed accordingly."

"Doctor," Pompey said. "I'm cousin to Poteet. Cade has just started with me. But I'd like to see about them both."

He studied Pompey a while. "You can see them, but don't stay long."

Pompey saw Ebb first, who was quiet, eyes closed. Pompey stood a while by his bed before heading to Zander, who was begging, "Pompey, please get me some water. I'm hurting bad. Horrible bad." But he was alert and clear-eyed as he was talking, which led Pompey to think it wasn't so very bad. Zander just needed to settle in a while. Let the healing get going as it should.

When he saw Helen later that evening, he told her about the wreck. "The other driver ran off before I even had a chance to talk to him." Helen thought he looked worried and said so.

"I need to keep track of Zander. His momma, Aunt Letitia, she's always been good to our family. It's least I could do. Can you help? He's in the Annex now, so it wouldn't take you long to go see him. You wouldn't miss much cleaning time."

"Pearlie and me clean the Annex, too. So, yeah, I'll look in on him. Probably have to clean up after him some." She nodded "I'll see about Zander for you."

So Helen and Pearlie looked in on Zander and Ebb every time they could manage it. Zander needed the most talking to. The most hand holding. But Helen could see him getting well pretty quick. Helen judged him to be happier in the hospital bed than on his own two feet. He was content to take his own sweet time getting well.

Ebb, he was doing all right, too, but was troubled most by the arthritis in his knees, which wasn't from the accident. Zander had got his broken bones set just an hour after he got to the Annex, but they waited two days before setting Ebb's legs. Pearlie told her, "These doctors know what they're doing. They got their reasons."

The main doctor, Hollister, came by while Pearlie was visiting with Ebb, and she felt awkward around the head man, so she moved away soon as Hollister started talking to Ebb. She was stripping a bed across from Zander. First Hollister talked about the arthritis. "That's going to take more time, Mr. Cade. We might have to give you some special medications. Some vaccinations. The injuries to your femur and patella might be problematic, so we'll need to collect some samples to study."

Ebb nodded put his hand up over his mouth, then said, "What kind of samples?"

"Not sure just yet. We'll certainly draw some blood. Do x-rays, too. We'll do some other tests, depending on how you do."

Dr. Friedkin walked up just then, and Dr. Carter came walking up, looking hard at Ebb. Pearlie couldn't think of anything wrong that Ebb had done, but Carter didn't look too happy. He was getting upset with Friedkin. "Doctor," Carter said. "I don't want to miss a chance to state my objections here." Now Friedkin's face was getting red, and Pearlie thought there might be some fireworks coming up. It was getting too crowded, so she took dirty sheets to the chute, and when she came back through the doctors were gone.

Later Helen told Pompey what Pearlie knew about Zander, and he grinned real happy, pulling her to him, squeezing her gratefully. "My sweetness," was all he said, making her wish they was already married. Not that they'd let her sleep with him. The CEW didn't allow Colored couples to stay together in The Pen. Just the women. Pompey lived in a trailer on the other side of Scarborough Village with four other men.

She asked him, "Do you think they'll run that White man off? Him that caused the wreck in the first place?"

He said. "White man runs into a Colored man. Who do you think they're going to blame? I just got to hope the boss man needs me doing these double shifts." Hearing this, Helen knew it was her turn to hug on him, whispering and calling his name, which was all he needed to hear. And he made sure she knew that's what he needed.

And the boss kept Pompey, Stanley, Lucas, and Big Alvin doing everything they'd already been doing. He told Pompey "When your other two boys get well, you can have them back. Meantime, just do your best."

One way or another Pompey got a report almost every day on Zander, and he was doing pretty good in two weeks. Cast on his left ankle. Ribs not so bad any more. You could tell he wanted to get back to drinking and carousing again. See some of the girls he'd been following around like a dog after her that's in heat. Helen and Pearlie called him Little Romeo.

On a Sunday Helen was in the Annex mopping when Zander came up on crutches. "Helen, they're letting me go from here." He was happy as he could be, adding, "Friedkin says I can't work just yet. Got to rest so the bones get stitched back together again. Stronger than before, but I won't be resting here. They won't pay me nothing, but I can eat for free. For a couple weeks maybe." He was more than ready to get back in circulation with the gals he used to know.

She finished mopping and went down to see about stripping his bed, and she saw Ebb still in his bed. "I thought you'd get gone soon as Zander. You got any idea when they'll let you go?"

He scratched his head. "Nope," he said. "They might have forgot about me. I mean, they give me shots every two or three days. Not sure what that's for. I feel poorly after them shots, but it goes away. I got used to it." He seemed puzzled at Zander's getting out when nothing was said about him getting out. She thought he was ready to get back on the water truck.

Helen listened close whenever she was around Friedkin or Hollister to see if they'd talk about Ebb. From what she could tell they'd decided to keep him a while on general principle. Carter would come by sometimes. Stop and pick up Ebb's chart and study it. The other doctors didn't talk much, but Dr. Carter, he'd ask Ebb, "How you doing today, Mr. Cade? How're your knees?"

Ebb always said, "Ready to go any time you say, doc." Helen heard him say that several times.

But nobody said when Ebb'd be going back to work. One day Friedkin looked at Ebb's teeth. "You got some decay here. Fairly serious. We'll need to pull some teeth so they won't infect the others. You want good teeth, don't you? A good smile?"

Ebb liked the way his mouth felt even if it was terrible looking, so he didn't answer, maybe thinking he wouldn't have to hide his mouth much longer.

Friedkin looked like he was going to say something else, but he didn't. Ebb looked anxious, probably thinking Friedkin would ask him once and for all if he'd let them take some of his teeth, but the doctor didn't wait to hear Ebb's answer, and they pulled teeth the very next day; nine in all, which was a surprise. The next day they took six more. But Ebb ended up with bridgework that looked much better, and gave him no trouble. He was tickled about that. But they didn't talk about letting him go, and they started having him piss in a bottle and do his other business in a bedpan. They got it from him and took it down the hall. Helen thought this was odd because his knees were better now. No problem, but they hadn't done anything about his broke leg. The doctors kept a hold of him nearly three more weeks. Dr. Clark came by several times to see about Ebb, and he asked Ebb, "Mr. Cade, when was it you signed off on your dental work?"

"Sign off, you say? I never did that. They just took the worst I had." She asked Cade about all this, and he gave her a shy smile. "I gained seven pounds since the accident. Food's better here than at Scarborough Cafeteria. I'm still wondering why they're keeping me so long. Doing nothing…well, that ain't right…Doing very little for my wrist and leg." And he held up his arm to show a wrapped forearm and wrist. Not a cast. "I use crutches to get down to the big windows at the other end of the hall. Hurts a bit, but I shift weight over to my other leg. Hollister seen me once and told me to get back into bed. So now I wait until no doctors or nurses are close by, and I sneak down to the big windows to see if the world's still turning without me." He looks down at his bandaged arm, then up to Helen. "That old world's still turning out there. And I'd like to turn with it."

At shift change she told Pearlie about talking with Ebb and how it certainly was a puzzle how he was treated. "Have you heard anything your own self about him?"

"Not on the floor," Pearlie said. "But I believe I've heard talk about him while I's in the Store Room. Listening through the walls. I hear his name every day or two. Pretty regular, actually."

"What are they saying about him?"

"Sounds like some kind of peppermint…or is it perry mint?"

"What are you saying? Peppermint?"

Pearlie waved her hands around, flustered. "Not really sure what it is they're saying. Something like the 'Cade perry mint.' And they're wondering how the forty-seven will travel. How much will remain. How he'll be affected. What forty-seven's going to do to him."

"Forty-seven? What are you talking about? Forty-seven what?"

"I think it's something like pull-only-yum forty-seven. Or maybe pal-own-eyum forty-seven. I got no real clue. That's just what they talk about. 'How the forty-seven's going to travel.'"

That sure was a puzzle. But by this point Pearlie was ready to go home, and Helen was summoned by Dr. Carter to clean up after two boys had thrown up on third floor. Helen wondered about the forty-seven stuff, and she made sure to listen on the floor and especially in the Store Room.

Nothing.

After twenty days Dr. Friedkin set Ebb's broken legs, both of them, one after the other, and they took some bone samples while they were at it. Ebb was feeling better now that his legs weren't moving in the wrong direction. And he told Helen he was feeling a little better about things in general, figuring he'd be let go in ten days or so. Maybe with a crutch.

One day Helen was in the ward when Clark told Ebb, "If your pain diminishes, and you can walk normally, you can get back to work in a couple months."

"Couple of months? Doc, I been here too long already. You all doing more to me than anybody else on this floor. In this whole Annex, this whole outfit. I'm hoping to be ready in a few days."

Dr. Clark looked like he was ready to ask some more questions. Or maybe explain to Ebb what was really going on, but he never did. Helen had to go clean in the big building a while, and when she came back to Ebb's bed, he looked awful grim, which wasn't something he'd showed before. Not when Helen was around. "I think they's some funny bidness going on with some of these doctors." Looked that way to Helen, too. Something wasn't right.

She kept stopping by to check on Cade every day, and he was doing good. They took off his leg casts, and he walked up and down the ward, a little smoother every time. Helen could see it in his face. He was chomping on the bit to get back to work. And she could see how being kept on bedrest might bother anybody who'd gone through what Ebb had. Nobody else was being treated like him.

Pearlie stayed after her shift to talk to Helen again, hurrying to share her news. "Goodness sakes, Pearlie! What's eating you?"

"I heard a big argument through the wall in the Store Room. Doctors, I think," she said. "It probably was Clark and Hollister, both of em fit to be tied. Clark kept asking things like, 'Did we get it in writing? Show me proof. I want to see it with my own eyes.'"

She was pretty near out of breath, and Helen said, "What did Hollister say?"

"He said, 'We talked with a relative on the phone. She gave permission.'"

"That gave Clark some pause," Pearlie said. "But he came back with 'Did we get consent from the patient's relative…in writing?'" And she looked back at Helen like that was end of the story.

"Did they?"

"Didn't sound like it," Pearlie said. "And that's when it got real hot. I'd heard more than I could stand to hear. They had to be fussing about Ebb Cade. Had to be. I didn't want to run into either of them in the hall. For sure, they'd see in my eyes that I heard it. I just had to tell somebody, and you're the somebody, which is good enough for me. I'm getting out of here." And she was gone to the buses.

The next shift lasted a long, long time for Helen. She saw Ebb twice, but he was sleeping like a baby, so she didn't bother him. When she got back to the hutment around eight o'clock next morning, Pearlie wasn't there, so she had everything to herself. But she couldn't just hit the sack herself, so she went to see if Pompey's truck was anywhere close. She walked around outside looking for him and found him a couple rows down. When he saw her, he headed to her, asking, "What is it, Sweetness? You looking for me?"

"You know Ebb Cade, right?"

"Sure. He got hurt in the wreck. I seen him most times when I went by to see Zander."

Helen said, "That's right. He's the one. They're not doing right by him." And she explained what Ebb had said about getting back to work. She told about the argument between Hollister and Clark. Took a while explaining about hearing voices through the Store Room wall.

Pompey drew her over to a couple of turned over water barrels where they could sit. He patted her knee and said, "Not sure I understand. Tell it to me again. All of it." And that was what she was hoping for. Pompey was good-hearted. He'd know what to do. But when she finished telling it all the way through again, he scratched his chin and neck slowly. "Go back to your hut, and I'll be there in half an hour, maybe sooner." She smiled quickly. "That's what I want."

"You might need to get things answered your own self. Not relying on Pearlie. She might have left something out. Might have misunderstood something. Let me think about the best way to go." They stood, and he kissed her like he meant to take her to bed soon as he could, which was how she kissed him, too. He patted her hip when she turned to go, and she almost stopped to go back, but he was already headed to the truck.

He was at her hutment in fifteen minutes and told Big Alvin," Go down the rest of this row, you and Stanley. Pick me up when you get to the next row. I got something to do here." After the truck was parked by the next hutment he said, "There's no telling what's going on with Cade. Might be some kind of secret."

Helen had heard the words secret now and then, but never let it concern her. She just went on with what she was cleaning. Didn't give it another thought. Which might be something she shouldn't have been doing.

"What kind of secrets?" she said.

"No idea. The CEW is partly construction, partly Army. Mostly factories and plants all set up for the War Effort."

"What do they make in the factories?"

"That," he said, "is what's secret. Me and you, we shouldn't even be talking about it." He got quiet and looked around for the truck, but didn't see or hear it. So he looked at her a while, and she did some thinking about the whole thing. Finally, she said, "So what do you think?"

He stood up and walked to look around the corner, then back again. Sat back down. "I'd keep my ears open to see what I could learn. But I wouldn't do anything else. We need to stay where we's supposed to stay. Just do your job. You're a good worker...."

"Just like you," she said.

He grinned. "I don't know how much longer I'll be doing two shifts, water and sewage. We don't want to mess all this up for us."

She liked that he kept saying *we*. He was being careful, trying to help her be careful, too. And that was a good thing. Nan and Pap would want that for her.

"All right, Honey. I can do what you're telling me." And she pulled him close to kiss him, and his hands lingering where she wanted him to linger. She didn't talk about how much she'd be listening to anything about Cade. How she'd be in the Store Room whenever there was a reason. How she'd do whatever Friedkin asked her to do. Maybe get close to Clark, if she could. But she didn't cotton getting close by Hollister, who never acknowledged any Negro, except to order them to do something. His voice sullen, as if it was the maid or orderly that had caused the problem in the first place. Helen Jones and Pearlie Booker cleaned up after mistakes Whites made every day. Every night. She realized that was a big part of why she was trying so hard to find out why Ebb was being done the way he was.

She worked slow whenever Clark or Friedkin was around, listening to what she could. She took a few extra minutes while she was in the Store Room and eventually figured out there was some kind of air duct between it and Hollister's office. Should have realized that sooner, but it didn't matter because her night shift work didn't line up much with Hollister who was a morning and daylight man, usually gone every afternoon by five or five-thirty. She told Pearlie to listen as often as she could, but her friend never had anything more to report.

Ebb was getting better. You could see it in his step after they took his casts off. They kept giving him a shot each week, and sometimes that gave him a headache. "I ain't never hurt in my head like I been hurting here," he said. But he never complained about the other things, diarrhea or when he had a stomach ache. "This ain't like me to be touchy after meals. Somehow I's lost the weight I gained." Helen noticed his gums would bleed just a tad after his supper sometimes. Not every night, but it was there. Maybe because all those teeth of his were gone.

Helen was working hard, and she got to fill in on a second shift for a White maid who left unexpected. Just walked away from the job. Friedkin tracked Helen down on the second floor, asking, "Can you do double shifts for us a while? We know of somebody who'll take the job, but she's working somewhere else til next Monday. I told Hollister I'd ask you. Just for four days." He was studying her face. "What do you think?"

She thought about the money and said, "I can do it. Four days and four nights, right?"

Dr. Friedkin held a piece of paper in his hand, and she could tell he had something else to do after connecting with her. Something about the paper maybe? So she said it again. "Four days and nights. When do I start? I can start tomorrow morning if that will help you."

He smiled. "That works for us, Helen. Are you sure it'll work for you? You'll need to pace yourself to make it through two shifts."

She smiled, thinking she'd talk with Pompey to get an idea how to make it through just as well as he did. *He's got some tricks to make it through two shifts out of three. He can teach me.*

So that perked her up some, which lasted about an hour. It was about 1:30 when she lost momentum and nearly ran out of gas. She was on the second floor mopping when she noticed someone approaching from down the hall. Dr. Friedkin looked to be in a hurry. Still holding the paper. "Have you seen Mr. Cade?"

"No, sir. Do you need him?"

"He's gone. Nobody knows where he is."

"You want me to help look for him?"

"I do. I'll look all through the Annex if you'll go look through the hospital. Negroes should be in the

Annex, of course, but it would be smart to check both places."

So that's how it went with her hurrying up and down through every hall. There weren't many empty rooms. Counting forty beds in the Annex, the CEW hospital had about three hundred beds, so it took a while. She asked at every nurse's station, but nobody had seen him. Friedkin found her after half an hour, and she told him she'd ask around, but nobody knew anything about Ebb Cade.

"I didn't get around to everybody in the Annex," he said. "Would you go ask on the third floor? I need to see Dr. Hollister in the morning, And I need to take some notes before I see him. Need to have things in order."

Helen went where she was directed. No luck. She went to Ebb's bed, which had not been slept in. It was made up neat as a pin. Nothing to indicate he'd been there for eight weeks. The ward was filled up, a man in every bed, all of them quiet. Asleep. She went back to her mop to finish where she'd been before searching for Ebb. Bad feeling about all this. About Ebb Cade.

Friedkin didn't get back to her until the next morning, surprising her as he walked up. "Helen, I thank you for your help, but I've got to see Hollister right now." He waved the paper as he said it. "There's no sign of Mr. Cade. A nurse said he'd been discharged."

"Well, no wonder we can't find him."

Friedkin shook his head. "He's my patient. He can't be discharged without my signing off on him." He shook his head slower. "I never signed off on Ebb Cade."

"I need to finish mopping here," she said. "But if you want me to, I'll keep on looking."

"No. You do what you need to do, and I'll do what I need to do." He glanced down at his piece of paper. Helen nodded. "Yes, sir."

They never did find Ebb. But after Helen worked from eleven at night until three that next afternoon, when she got back to the hutment she had a little trouble getting to sleep. Just flat out overtired. Pearlie'd been working with her from seven in the morning til three in the afternoon, and she wanted to talk, but Helen was too tired to listen. She managed to explain about Ebb's disappearing from the Annex, and naturally Pearlie was wanting to know more. Helen said, "When we get back on the bus, I'll tell you what I know. I got to sleep now."

That helped a good bit, and while they were on the bus Pearlie was pretty good about just listening, asking only a few questions, which Helen thought was sweet of her because she herself would ask dozens of questions. When they got to the hospital, Pearlie said, "I'll start off on the first floor. You go start in the Annex." First thing Helen checked Ebb's bed and found another guy in it. She asked him, "Did they tell you anything about the man who had this bed yesterday?"

He shook his head, couldn't answer her. One sick fellow.

Around halfway through the morning shift Pearlie came to find Helen. "You might want to check the message board when you get a chance. Over at the front door."

"What's going on?"

"Just go look."

The message board was brand new. Hollister's idea, but Clark had been the one pushing it. "It's a good way to get people to stay on top of changes. New regs, new procedures and protocol. We need everybody to know what's changing around here, which seems to happen every day." Hollister added, "I like it. Nobody can say 'I didn't know.' We'll put it on the main hall where everybody signs in. Anyone who doesn't read we shouldn't have hired in the first place."

Helen had to fetch some new linens anyway, and she was curious about what Pearlie was talking about. She stopped at the reception desk, asking, "Can I leave these linens with you a minute? I want to read the message board."

The White gal said, "Sure. Go ahead. And watch out for Dr. Friedkin if you can. Dr. Hollister wants to see him about something. He had a big meeting with him. It was some kind of fracas. Some kind of ultimatum."

"Ulta what?"

The receptionist said, "That's what Friedkin called it after they had their meeting. He was talking with somebody else, and I heard him say, 'Hollister better do as promised. I gave him an ultimatum. General Groves has agreed. Now it's going to be law!'" Her face was flushed as she told it, and Helen wanted to know more, but it was more important to go see the thing for herself. It was just around the corner at the sign in board.

REGULATION---JUNE 3, 1945

We believe that no substance known to be, or suspected of being, poisonous or harmful should be given to human beings unless the following conditions are fully met: (a) that a reasonable hope exists that the administration of such a substance will improve the condition of the patient, (b) that the patient gave his complete and informed consent in writing, and © that the responsible next of kin give in writing a similarly complete and informed consent, revocable at any time during the course of such treatment.

Helen went back through the notice three more times, reading slowly so she could understand it good herself and so she could tell Pompey. She worked the double shift, wondering about Ebb. Where he was now? How did he get away? What he was doing? She had heard Dr. Clark say Ebb was 53 years old, so how was the old man getting on? And her mind came back to Ebb at odd times. It was like he was her kin, some beloved uncle who had gone off to something better than we got here. Maybe something not paying as much as the CEW paid, but something honest and careful and good for all of us. But nothing else came of Ebb except for Helen's wondering if that forty-seven had hurt him somehow. Rumors went around about Ebb Cade, but nobody ever knew for sure what happened to him.

Five months later she told Pompey she didn't want to wait much longer. They didn't know of any Colored churches around CEW, but she told him, "We can go off down by the river a while. We know what to do, don't we?" and she stared into his face a while, waiting for him to say something. He smiled, but didn't say anything. She added "We don't have to tell nobody for a while, but we can jump the broom ourselves, and tell the world another time."

"Sweet!" he said. And they did what she said. After two weeks she told Pearlie, which let the whole world know they were married. Didn't change much else. And the double shifts went away. More and more people found the CEW. There was plenty of coming and going.

So things rumbled along as the hustle and bustle spread through the whole outfit, the whole CEW, and in early 1946 there was a big to do about the Cade situation. She didn't get all the details because, of course, some of it was secret. She heard nurses gossiping about the forty-seven. They said it was deadly. It could settle in the teeth and bones. One nurse said it was horrible poisonous; the other said it was radioactive. Helen didn't know about radios, but whatever it was those nurses were spooked about the forty-seven. Helen remembered Hollister wanting to know how it traveled. He was anxious about it, like it was an evil, living thing growing out of control in anyone unlucky to carry it. Like the guy named Ebb Cade, who didn't deserve what was given to him. Whites had shared it with Coloreds, and no matter what they said, it wasn't good for anything. It could turn deadly. It was terrible filth that she, Pearlie, Pompey, and his men needed to clean up wherever it was hiding.

She realized she'd done all that scrubbing, mopping, and scraping during her time at the hospital and learned there's a few things in this world that leave permanent stain. Some, brand new, not yet known.

Silver

At 0700 hours Theo Kincaid walked down the short hall, careful with the long-corded phone, calling out to General Groves, "Colonel Kenneth Nichols holding for you, sir." The General spat toothpaste into the sink, tapping his toothbrush firmly three times, stepped out into the hall, and took the phone.

"Thank you, Kincaid. Now I need some privacy."

Kincaid headed back toward the kitchen.

Groves knew Nichols had met yesterday with the Undersecretary of the Treasury, Daniel Bell. This call would report the results of that very important conversation. Groves had needed to shift his schedule slightly because he'd begun his day with another phone call about the latest financial update for the CEW. Captain Hubbell was due to arrive at Hackworth House in ten minutes, bringing information about a personnel issue, but all that could wait until Groves heard from Nichols.

The government operated on a priority system when purchasing supplies and materials, and Groves' priority was the very highest. He got first shot at whatever was available every time he went shopping. The only way he came back empty-handed was if there was nothing left to buy. Given the status of the War, several critical commodities were already in short supply. Copper was quite scarce, and, even though copper would be essential for certain Y-12 tasks, Groves had been completely shut out of procuring copper, which was critical for encapsulating materials used in the isotope separation process. This frustrated the General for nearly a day and a half until he learned that silver was a viable substitute for copper, and that the country had tons of silver hidden away in vaults at West Point. The country's caches of gold and silver backed all the currency in circulation, which ought to have prevented Groves from acquiring it. In fact, Bell had protested loudly that the Treasury would never risk bankrupting the country by giving away its gold and silver. Groves had countered, saying he didn't need to keep the silver. "I just want to borrow it for a while," he'd told Nichols. "I'll give it all back…eventually."

Bell wanted to know exactly what the silver would be used for. "That would help me make a decision." But Groves answered, "I cannot give you that information. It's Top Secret." Bell hadn't been pleased to hear that, but Groves didn't relent. "We need the silver if we intend to win this War. That's all I can tell you. All you need to know."

While Bell had promised to give Groves an answer within twenty-four hours, he had failed to meet the deadline, and that was what Groves discussed with Nichols. "Get an appointment with somebody else at Treasury," he'd said. "Go as high as you can up the ladder and impress upon them that we want use of about fifteen thousand tons of silver. If Bell hears that we're prepared to go around him, that might motivate him to answer. Stress that we'll send it all back after we eliminate Hitler and Tojo."

Nichols felt like he'd hit a brick wall with Bell, and had brought up several potential problems and sticking points he anticipated when he'd be meeting with Treasury officials, but Groves had answers for every one of them. He said, "Our Top Priority Status addresses that. Remind them we're at the absolute top. Keep reminding them. The President has greased the tracks for us whenever we need something. And, by God, we need that silver!"

Nichols said, "I'll do what I can."

The General didn't appreciate that kind of attitude, that choice of words. "Listen," he told Nichols. "I'll call a few senators and get them to push Treasury on our behalf. I'll talk with Speaker McCormack about it, and Senator McKellar, too. He'll want Tennessee to get everything needed for the project. I'll phone Morganthau and Stimson as well, so that's the Speaker of the House, a senator from Tennessee, the Secretary of War, and the Secretary of the Treasury. If we make sure they understand we'll be returning the silver, they'll come around. I'll get Stimson to put some pressure on Bell, too. Make him understand depriving us of this loan could jeopardize the War Effort. If we don't achieve our goal, the Germans could develop something worse than what we're working on. We could lose the War, for God's sake!"

As agitated as he seemed, Groves finally said, "All right, Kenneth. We've got a plan. I'll make my calls. You go talk with the Higher Ups at Treasury---Bell, if you can. If he won't see you today, let Harry Hopkins know. Hopkins is Roosevelt's oldest confidant, and the President has told me Harry can speed things up. He knows everybody. I want to hear from you with an update before 1000 hours today and same time tomorrow. We need that silver!"

There was a knock at the front door. Without moving, Groves raised his voice, "Come in, Hubbell, come in." Then he told Nichols, "10 A.M. we'll talk again." And he hung up.

Clyde Hubbell, the Director of Intelligence for the Clinton Engineer Works had been on the job since November, 1942, less than a year. He was a 47 year-old, heavy-set man, with thinning, sandy-colored hair, a square jaw and pale blue eyes. Groves saw him as a man who listened first and asked questions later, which suited the General just fine.

While Groves sat on the sofa, Hubbell stood, outlining the situation. "Dr. Solomon Page is the subject, Ph.D. in physics. Thirty-four years old, single. Worked briefly at Harvard and at Berkeley. Robert Oppenheimer vouches for him. Here's his photograph. We're still gathering information about him. Father, mother, family. This photo's recent."

Groves studied the photo. "Doesn't look unstable to me. Clean cut, according to regulation, which is more than I can say for most of our scientists," Groves grumbled. "But what's he wearing? Why the headgear?"

Hubbell's voice shifted slightly, down a notch, more confidential. "That's part of what we're dealing with."

"I can live with the cap. We can overlook it." He turned back to the photo. "Still, it's odd, isn't it?"

"We've double-checked the various calculations he's done on the isotopes, and he's right on the money every time. Here's what's amazing---he's doing all the calculations in his head…faster and more accurately than other team members who use paper and pencil and the occasional slide rule. The man's truly exceptional. A mathematical genius. We need men like Page."

"He feels Page has a deep psychosis, possibly related to the serious injuries suffered by three of his colleagues in a laboratory accident. Dr. Page began wearing the baseball cap that very day. After two days he shifted into overdrive, pulling an all-nighter, to finish up a critical computation that impressed Oppenheimer so much that he suggested making Page a team leader. When we mentioned the baseball cap, Oppenheimer requested Page come see him in person. Spend some time together talking privately. I expect his concerns are similar to yours. I'm not sure about him. I have a feeling there's something else we haven't discovered. But he does have Oppenheimer in his corner."

"I remember Oppenheimer's request," Groves said. "I denied it. No reason to take Page away from his team. And now that I know what you've just told me I'm certain I made the right decision."

Groves stared out the window a moment, then said, "Page's too important to the project simply to send him to the Funny Farm. It would slow us down too much to replace him and bring his replacement up to speed."

"That's why we've been so cautious in approaching him about his cap. On the one hand, it's a minor quirk. On the other hand, why's it so important that he won't take it off? Something's not right there. We don't want to drive him over the edge. We don't know if he suspects what we're doing to analyze him. Or if he…if he's really…."

"Nuts," Groves said. "If he's really nuts."

"Exactly," Hubbell said. "We need more time with him."

"Might not be able to afford more time," Groves said.

Groves looked again at the photograph. "I want to meet him myself," he said. "Where are we holding him?"

"At the Hospital Annex, third floor."

"Have you seen him today?"

Hubbell shook his head. "He was having breakfast when I went by. I didn't speak with him."

"What sort of security is present at the annex?"

"We have MP's assigned to him, two in the main room where he spends most of the day. There are other patients in and out. We've explained to Page the MP's are orderlies…that's what we call them…but I think he knows they're there for him, not patients in general. We said they're there to prevent sabotage. They eat and sleep at the annex. The patient's rooms have solid oak doors, bars at the windows. Discreet but sufficient to prevent unauthorized exits."

Groves nodded. "I see."

Hubbell said, "He's given us no reason to increase security, sir." He brought a cigar out of a pocket. "May I?"

The General waved a hand. "Certainly." Then he tapped the photograph. "I see no good reason for his baseball cap. If he gets pushed on that, which he will sooner or later, would he resist?"

"Burgess and Setzer see no indication he'd become combative," Hubbell said.

"Still, I want the security presence increased," Groves said. "Three men on duty at all times. They don't have to hold his hand when he urinates, but I've known of men using their bathroom breaks to do themselves serious harm. I was present in Panama when a fellow broke a window and used the glass splintered fragments to slash both wrists. He bled out in eight minutes. We had a carpenter at the Pentagon who went completely off his nut. Took six MP's to subdue him. We had a psychiatrist working with him. Thought he was going to be okay…until he jumped out a third story window. Took the psychiatrist with him. Both dead when they hit the ground."

Hubbell exhaled smoke overhead. "We can come up with some plausible explanation for changing the protocols. Tell him there have been additional threats to the isotope project because that's God's honest truth. Explain that we're taking new steps to keep him safe."

"Which, indeed, we are," Groves said. "Handle it so that he doesn't feel threatened. That could add to his paranoia." Groves leaned back to stare at the ceiling. "In a way, we're protecting him from himself, but it's a good strategy just now for him to believe we're protecting him from an external enemy. Tell him the extra security is required. How it's justified to Page, that's their call. Set up a meeting with them in advance of my meeting today with Page. Let's make it..." He glanced at his watch. "Make it at 1400 hours for the psychiatrists. I want to see Page by 1550. I may or may not actually speak with him, depending on what Burgess and Setzer tell me. I don't want to lose an important asset, but neither do I want to keep an unstable personality on the team. We need to be one hundred percent sure he's able to withstand the stress of the race we're in. I'll make my decision about him today."

"Yes, sir," Hubbell said. "We need to proceed cautiously on this one."

"We need to do that on everything, Clyde. Everything we do. Just because we can get the resources we want doesn't mean we can't be whipped. The Japs are using something called a banzai charge, where they go for broke, throwing every man they have into desperate, often suicidal charges against larger enemy positions. And sometimes that banzai approach works. We need to be ready for anything Felix Robert Page does." He ran his hand through his hair. "Let's get something we can work with now. As soon as possible. Today would be best."

Hubbell left soon afterward, and the General summoned his driver, Brummett, and they left Hackworth House for X-10 where he took a tour of the graphite reactor and met with a team of technicians reviewing the new cooling procedures required for enhancing uranium. Groves asked questions, at times cutting off answers before the respondent had concluded. There were a few disgruntled expressions, wrinkled brows, glares of irritation. He didn't acknowledge them because they weren't relevant. Groves knew the salient issues were always operational. Can we get it done or not? Yes or no? Can we just get something operational now and save the improvements for later? Can we make any progress now? Today?

Groves was sometimes tempted to give too much information to individuals whose reputations were beyond question. When he did so, he always stressed that the Manhattan Project extended far beyond the Clinton Engineer Works. He was frequently tempted to lay out everything he'd arranged for the project's success, but there was danger in that because the scientists would then ask questions, some of which he probably couldn't answer, and, even if he could answer them, they'd want to discuss the theoretical implications of the science. Dick Groves got the impression that scientists in general reacted to new information as if they were entertaining one another at a cocktail party, speculating endlessly back and forth about minor details. Splitting theoretical hairs. They weren't driven to succeed, and they didn't owe allegiance to military timetables and objectives.

The Manhattan Project was comprised of other similar sites, forming a grander scheme than any one uninformed person could imagine. These components were located in several scattered, and in some cases remote spots around the country, New Mexico, Chicago, New York, and Washington state. In that respect the Manhattan Project was a massive undertaking. Yet each site was completely compartmentalized and separate from its relatives. Conceptually, the General found it challenging in its complexity, requiring constant singularity of vision and monitoring. He drove and pushed everyone to do his best, and sometimes he found himself wondering if he was handling everything properly. For Groves it always came down to the same decision: should he drive the team to achieve more, to work harder and faster, to strive for more than he had charged them with? Or should he praise the leaders, noting that they'd already exceeded his expectations, hoping and praying they'd actually fulfill the objectives he'd outlined? No, that wasn't it. Time was the real problem. The project's AAA rating could not give him more time.

In the long run Groves always demanded more of himself and more of everyone he dealt with. Somehow he felt he hadn't yet arrived at the best method for coordinating the work. Try as he might, he hadn't found a way to persuade the intellectuals to get on with the work he'd assigned them. "Don't ask questions," he said. "Do the task assigned." He'd tell them if he felt they needed a wider perspective, additional information, or more material and equipment. He didn't explain much. If a man couldn't deal with that, the General fired him and found somebody else who could do the work assigned.

But could that work this time with this Page fellow?

Time and again Groves had deliberately made begrudging accommodations for failure and delay, both of which were pure anathema to his "can-do" style. At the same time, the notion that it was possible to create a superweapon transforming uranium into something so powerful it could destroy the entire planet---that idea was daunting. Germany's pursuit of that idea and Britain's, too, led to intense competition. Who knew if Russia was likewise interested? The General felt all the pressure of a rapidly developing arms race of tremendous proportions. A German scientist named Von Braun had sped up the race by developing long-range rockets so that bombs could be delivered from hundreds or even thousands of miles away. Fortunately, the Allies had spirited Von Braun away from the Nazis, and he was continuing his work for the US now.

Von Braun's work complemented the work of Robert Oppenheimer, who, along with Edward Teller, Rudolph Peierls, and several other top scientists, had developed a theoretical model of something termed an "atomic bomb." This weapon was theoretically more powerful than thousands of tons of traditional high explosives. One such bomb could devastate an entire city. Groves was still awed by the potential effectiveness of these weapons, but he was just as frustrated and wary of what could happen accidentally as the US raced recklessly to create such a weapon. Groves was obsessed with the question of what would happen if the reaction necessary to refine uranium, which was the raw material needed to build these weapons…what if it couldn't be halted? If it could not be somehow restrained? There were some scientists who postulated that this weapon would explode repeatedly and exponentially until the entire atmosphere of earth would incinerate. Would the man who used such a weapon destroy the earth and life as we know it?

Groves telephoned and interrogated Oppenheimer and his cronies several times a week to learn as much as he could about the science behind the weapon, and a nagging unanswered question returned again and again. Oppenheimer called this concept a "chain reaction," a self-sustaining series of reactions, one leading to another, which, in turn, leads to yet another ad infinitum. A series of self-amplifying explosions everywhere.

Will an atomic bomb continue growing and reacting forever? Or is there some self-limiting aspect to the reaction that can be molded, aimed, and controlled merely to harm the enemy instead of enemy plus bomb maker, too? These questions haunted Groves, but he never acknowledged publicly any doubts about what he was doing. After all, he was authorized by the President to seek answers and build the weapon before Germany did. That was his charge. Groves had come to know President Roosevelt better as they communicated by mail, telephone, and on a few occasions in person, and he trusted Roosevelt just as he feared what might occur if the madman, Adolph Hitler, got answers before the Allies did. Roosevelt's foresight had inculcated in Groves a resourcefulness that knew no bounds. Roosevelt had said, "For God's sake, do everything you can to beat Hitler on developing this weapon. We cannot lose this race."

Therefore, Dick Groves went all out. He wasn't waiting passively for the scientific community to learn through trial and error some sure, safe way to create this superweapon. He had heard the physicists debating among themselves. He had learned about graphite reactors, electromagnetic separation, and gaseous diffusion. Each method could be the final answer, but which one would it be---and when?

Instead of waiting to see which method was most effective, he had pushed them all to the top, operationalizing all three almost simultaneously. The graphite alternative was already in place here at X-10; the electromagnetic isotope method was now installed at Y-12; and the gaseous diffusion method, if it could be used at all, would be born here at the CEW, too. All of the methods entailed risks and outright danger to personnel, but Groves was especially wary of gaseous diffusion because the gas itself was so corrosive that it literally ate through the thickest steel piping encasing it, and that apparently was what paralyzed Dr. Page. What did Page know the General didn't?

He kept remembering the face of a young technician whom he had met and chatted with on one of his tours in Chicago where they were testing a prototype for gaseous diffusion which involved the toxic uranium hexafluoride. That face, he recalled, belonged to a fine young man, enthusiastic about his work, confident they'd succeed and win the war, a fellow Groves would have been proud to call his own son. His name was Michael Sears. The General had decided to keep track of Mike, perhaps getting him transferred to the CEW. However, two days after Groves had visited with him there was an accident, a leak in the pipes Sears was monitoring, and he got caught in the pressurized, high temperature spray caused by a microscopic pinhole in the pipe. His fellow technicians had not been able to extract him promptly from the spray, and he died less than an hour later. Radioactivity had destroyed his skin cells and his brief exposure to the toxic hexafluoride had created deeper burns below the skin level which destroyed tissue at an astonishing rate. Sears never regained consciousness, which the doctors said was a blessing. The radioactive material literally consumed his body from the inside out. That was hexafluoride---the terrifying stuff they'd be handling and experimenting with.

Nichols called back. "Bell's in with Stimson as we speak," he said. "I'm pretty sure McKellar's met with him, too. McKellar was in the hall before I entered Bell's outer office."

"What did McKellar tell you?"

"Nothing, but he looked like the cat that swallowed the canary."

They talked a while longer, but Nichols had no other news. Groves repeated his directive. "Keep me informed. I'll be in meetings this afternoon, so call me to report around 1800 hours. And keep pushing Bell. Push him, push him, and push him.

Revelations

Bathsheba Miriam Markley Kincaid preferred her nickname Bashie, given to her by her husband Theo. He doted on her, often sneaking up behind her to hug her, kissing her neck, which always made her shudder with sudden pleasure. She fussed at him, "Theo, stop. You know I can't…" But she never finished explaining because she always wriggled around to look him in the eye, frowning and smiling simultaneously when she saw his grin. He loved her and was trying to buck up her feelings. To help her be happy.

"I can't help it, Hedy. You're too delicious to ignore." And this very predictable reply embarrassed her even more because he likened her to the movie star, Hedy Lamarr, whose brown eyes, long silken tresses, and slender frame made her one of the most popular romantic leads in Hollywood. Lamarr was an exquisite almost feline creature. Being compared to her made Bashie self-conscious, but because Theo reminded her over and over, she had to forgive him for feeling the way he did. This was especially true since she'd got sick eight months previous with whatever it was that afflicted her. The doctors had not identified her malady, which had caused a miscarriage and a later a stillbirth. She was desperate for a child while he was desperate for her. They had gone to church over this, but that hadn't helped, which really shook her to the core. But a friend had mentioned a new church, a freewill Baptist place. Not an established, formidable sect. Something brand new and very much out of the ordinary. Bashie had been so shaken over the past year she decided to go see what it was like. She hadn't mentioned anything to Theo, who thought she was at a doctor's appointment instead of gone to see what this new approach to religion might be. This new avenue to faith and redemption.

So there she was. Bashie recognized the gap in the cedars where she was supposed to go, but she didn't like the looks of it. It was well inside the city limits of North Clinton, but it felt like it was way out in the country. The kudzu here was thick, and the branches hung low, camouflaging what must be the path to the house, but she couldn't be certain of that. She walked ahead, pushing through the branches to find that the path wound around a little. She edged through, easing along the path for about twenty yards all told, coming out into a small clearing where the house was, a small, boxy place with a mossy, shingled roof and mildew-stained siding. This place, deep in shadow.

Approaching the front door, Bashie saw a handwritten sign *Foot of the Cross Church* at the same time that she became aware of voices inside. She was about to knock on the door when it suddenly opened, and a man wearing a white dress shirt, thin dark tie, and dark navy trousers exited the building. His thinning, sandy-colored hair and receding chin gave him a timid, wary look. As he gestured that she should enter, she did just that, and he followed close behind. He spoke to a small group of people who were apparently waiting for him. "Find your seats. We're just about to start. There's still room for anyone seeking the true word of God."

The room was perhaps twenty feet by twelve. A bare, wooden floor, two windows along one wall, and nothing else to speak of except mismatched ladder-back chairs laid out in three rows facing the opposite wall. Nearly half the seats were occupied. Some of the audience were working folk who appeared to have put in a full day's labor before coming to what might be termed a camp meeting. Bashie took a seat on the back row as the fellow who'd followed her in strode to the front of the room.

"Greetings," he said in a voice that filled the room. "I see new faces here tonight. In addition, I see some others who have professed their faith in days past." He stepped toward a fellow seated on the front row, a large man wearing a battered straw hat, bib overalls, and muddy brogans. The speaker offered his hand, which was taken up eagerly. "Mr. Hatmaker, you're always welcome here, but where is your good wife tonight?"

"Stayed in Lake City, looking after her sister who's took sick. She ast me to make apologies for her, Mr. Hensley."

"Not necessary a tall. We hope to see her return next time we're all together," Hensley said, moving to the next man on the row. "Mr. Leinart, how are you this evening?"

"Just fine, sir."

Hensley continued in this fashion, speaking to each in turn. When he encountered two women near the window, he said, "You're new here, sisters. Thank you for coming. How should I call you when we speak?"

These women, dressed in coarse, beige, shapeless shifts and clunky, black, old-fashioned shoes, were obviously related. Short brown hair cut severely at the neck, brown eyes, noses flattened as if God had mashed them back into their faces at birth. Not pretty, but striking and memorable. The larger of the two said, "I'm Sally Fisher. This here's my sister, Nell."

"And why is it you've come?"

"To hear The Word and see the Proof of Faith," Nell said.

This reply seemed to give Hensley something to think about because he ended his interview right there even though he hadn't made it all round the room. Instead, he made his way back to the front, and, when he turned to face his congregation again, he had changed somehow. Raising both hands toward the ceiling, he asked, "How many of us have felt the hand of the Oppressor?" A few hands went up, but this apparently disappointed him. He pointed to Hatmaker, his voice rising as he said, "Brother Hatmaker, tell us what the Oppressor has took from you and your family. Tell about your punishment."

Hatmaker shifted in his chair so he faced the group. His cheek splotched red as he spoke. "Back in '36 the Government took our farm for Norris Dam," he muttered. "And," he said, "they didn't pay us what our place was worth. Not even close. Swindled us was what they did. Plain and simple."

"So you moved?" Hensley asked. "Where was you at? Where'd you end up?"

"Had two hundred thirty-five acres of good bottom land in Campbell County where part of Norris Lake is now," he said bitterly. "They drownded our farm right quick. We moved to Lake City where my wife's people's at. Just west of the creek. I work a mine up near Jellico, and let me tell you, I wadn made for mining. Don't care for that kind of work one little bit. I never would of chose mining. No, sir. Our life is sunk damned low, that's for sure."

"Yours is a common complaint," Hensley said. "I've heard this same kind of story from folks in Jacksboro and LaFollette. Big Government didn't do local folks much good with Norris Dam. Anyone else here who's been oppressed some other way? If so, I want to hear about it. All of us here, we want to hear about it, don't we?"

A chorus of grumbling resentment resulted as Nell Fisher waved her hand at Hensley, and he responded with, "Tell your story, Sister Fisher."

Nell stood up and said, "Me and Sally come over from North Carolina. Our family got oppressed something terrible by the Great Smokey Park." She let that air out for everybody a while. "A few years back the Government tooken our land, too. Run us off from just north of Bryson City where Daddy had his sawmill. Told us we had to get out for the national park they was starting. Daddy was paid barely forty cent on the dollar instead of true value. Sally and me, we took care of Mommy and Daddy nearly twelve year afore they passed. Daddy had tried that dimestore in Bryson City, but, when he died, we didn't have no idea how to keep it running. He didn't leave us no finance books, and we didn't know who to pay or who to report to the sheriff. We lasted but two and a quarter years afore we had to sell out. That was in 1939. We moved to Morrisville for a little while in 1941, a month before Pearl Harbor. Then to Fountain City in 1943. Now here in '44 we're working at Magnet Mills, both of us. Just barely getting by. Tried to get jobs in the Clinton Engineer Works, but they don't like us enough to hire us. The bastards."

She halted a moment, looking to her sister. Then she said, 'We're just poor as any old church mouse nowadays."

And her sister chimed in, "We lost nearly everything our family owned, and that ain't right!" Her voice, tinged with bitterness.

Another female hand went up. A small woman waving a piece of paper.

"Hello," Hensley said, approaching her. She handed him the paper, explaining, "I'm Shirley Morrow, and I got this letter last November. This here letter tells my story." She gave off a quiet intensity that surprised Bashie. With her gray hair captured in a bun, she seemed older than the rest, and to Bashie she seemed better off, better dressed than the others.

Hensley scanned the page and returned it to her. "You sure you want everybody to hear this, Mrs. Morrow?"

"I am."

"Maybe it would be better if you read it," Hensley said.

She shook her head. "I don't read so good. You ast about the Oppressor. The way I see it, this letter was writ by him. Read it aloud, and all of us will hear him speak. Read it out."

Hensley moved back to the front of the room. "Okay. It says

WAR DEPARTMENT

CORPS OF ENGINEERS

KINGSTON DEMOLITION RANGE

LAND ACQUISITION SECTION

HARRIMAN, TENNESSEE

November 11, 1942

Shirley Morrow

Rt. 1,

Oliver Springs, Tenn.

The War Department intends to take possession of your farm December 1, 1942. It will be necessary for you to move, not later than that date.

In order to pay you quickly, the money for your property will be placed into the United States Court at Knoxville, Tennessee.

The Court will permit you to withdraw a substantial part of this money without waiting. This may be done without impairing your right to contest the value fixed on your property by the War Department.

It is expected that your money will be put in court within ten days, and as soon as you are notified, it is suggested you get in touch with the United States Attorney to find out how much can be drawn.

Your fullest cooperation will be material aid to the War Department.

Very Truly Yours

Alton LeSieur

Project Manager

Somebody muttered, "Damn!"

Mrs. Morrow stood up, clutching a black pocketbook in front of her. "I bought my place just the other side of Black Oak Ridge just fifteen months ago.

Before that I was in Campbell County, but not anywhere close to the lake. Thought I was safe from getting removed for Norris Dam, but they came back and said they had miscalculated and needed my property. I wadn happy about that, so I ast who I could talk to. They pointed me toward LeSieur, but he don't listen a tall. Just nods his head and says I can appeal to the US Attorney in Knoxville. I tried that, too, but didn't get nowhere. Now I'm staying in Claxton, walking down the highway to get to work cleaning rooms at the Sleepy Time Motor Court. Me, I'm Freewill Baptist, but I heard about you, Mr. Hensley," she said earnestly. "And I need a Higher Power than what I see regular, so I come to watch and listen to the goings on here. And to pray for deliverance."

Hensley nodded solemnly, returning the letter. "Thank you, Sister Morrow. Thank you very kindly. You can set back down now."

Unconsciously, Bashie shook her head, thinking, *Mrs. Morrow's just plain unlucky,* but, as thoughts came into her head, she also recalled her husband's comment. One Theo had repeated more than once. "I guess I been luckier than most. I haven't been touched by misfortune. I was removed for Norris Dam, too, so I know how being removed can turn everything upside down. I'm awful lucky to be employed as caretaker at the Hackworth House where soldiers stay off and on.

But General Groves stays there more than anyone else. I run the place, keep it clean, cook meals for visitors. If you think about it, that's some pretty good luck." Bashie didn't have his faith and optimism.

Hensley was talking now. "I ain't lost what you all have lost, yet still I am your brother. I offer help. I offer solutions to these problems you've brought with you. But I am only one man. Solving your problems will require efforts of a vast multitude, and it will be a fierce struggle for us to succeed. We will, all of us, need to fight long and hard. We must be monstrous fierce. In fact, we may need to transform ourselves into something just as monstrous as our opponents in order to conquer the minions of evil. And you all know who the evil ones are, don't you? You've told stories about what the evil monsters took from you. You've brought letters signed by evil. An unsympathetic force, Big Government that tramples rough shod over our dreams."

Hensley had been pacing back and forth as he preached, increasing his volume as well as his pace, getting worked up about injustice that was known as Big Government.

"The callous fiend we know as Big Government is sometimes known by its initials," he said. "Ye shall know him by the letters FDR. Our so-called leader, Franklin Delano Roosevelt. Or by the initials TVA.

Tennessee Valley Authority. Or even by CEW. Clinton Engineer Works." His face was flushed with emotion and rhetoric.

"Those known merely by their initials are under the impression they're fundamentally superior to common people. It's as though we've been ordered not to speak the Devil's name. But I know him. He is FDR and TVA. Now he has become CEW! How despicable! How low and mean and horrible is all of this satanic chaos all around us! And how ripe these demons are for the fall! But, you know, they got the upper hand on all of you. Seems to me that at the CEW local folks like you here in East Tennessee don't seem to count for much."

"You damn right!" Hatmaker yelled. "They been treating us like shit!"

Hensley turned his back on the crowd, and all went quiet. When he turned around, his voice was softer, quieter, but his eyes were alert and brighter than before. He said, "There's Yankees and foreigners moved in all around us. Jews is taking all the best jobs at CEW. Jews, foreigners, and scientists thick as thieves in the CEW. And Big Government has forgot all about you folks. I say," he said, his voice louder now, "it's high time somebody got their attention. High time somebody reminded them who they work for. High time somebody took a stand and slowed down all this secrecy and destruction and foolishness they call the War Effort."

He stood looking from face to face, his breathing subsiding slowly, as though he had run a long way to bring them such news.

Sally raised her hand tentatively and asked, "But don't we want to win the War? They keep saying all this condemnation of property, all the removal of good country folk from their rightful homeplaces, all this infernal secrecy...all this is for the so-called War Effort. So we can beat the Japs and Krauts. That's what they tell us."

Hensley asked the group, "Does anyone here know what it is they're doing at CEW? Does anyone know what they're building? What they're making? Why is every damn thing a secret? Why won't they tell us anything?" He held his arms wide, gesturing as he asked, "Why don't they trust us? Why do they just take and take and take, not giving anything back? What is it they're hiding from us?"

Bashie felt her face get hot as she considered these questions, worried she and Theo were working for the wrong people at Hackworth House. Hensley just might be right, and people like General Groves somehow wrong. She surveyed the crowd, wondering if anyone else felt as conflicted as she did.

"Now is the time," Hensley said quietly. "Let me show you something, and then you will understand. I promise you that. It will all become clear in your mind." With that, he exited through a door behind him. The Fisher sisters found each other's hands, whispering back and forth. Then Hensley was back, carrying a wooden crate about 24 inches square, which he placed on an empty chair on the front row. "The twelfth chapter of Revelations tells a story," he said. "Does anyone here know it well enough to tell it? To share it with all of us here?"

No hands went up. Hensley smiled and said, "Then I will tell the story, brethren. And I will show you how strong you have to be to live by God's word as it is revealed in Revelations. Then you will understand why we're here tonight." He turned to Hatmaker, who had inched closer to the box. "Let me handle this," he muttered.

Hatmaker nodded soberly as Hensley addressed the group, "The story I'm telling is only part of a bigger story. We don't know the end of the story because it's happening right here in Anderson County. It's happening to us now. It's still happening."

Sally said, "I don't get what you're saying. Revelations is in the Bible, writ a long, long time ago. What do you mean it's happening now?"

Hensley's smile got strained a bit, but he sounded patient. "In Revelations it says there once was a woman in heaven, clothed with the sun, with the moon under her feet and a crown of stars on her head. She was going to have a baby, and, when she was about to deliver the child, she cried out in pain. While she was delivering the child, another sign appeared in the heavens. An enormous red Dragon with seven heads, ten horns, and seven crowns on its heads. The Dragon stood before the woman ready to devour her baby when it was born, but the baby was snatched up to be near God's throne, and a war broke out in heaven pitting Angels against the Dragon. There was rejoicing in heaven when the Dragon was vanquished. But..." his voice rising, "as a result of the battle, woe to the earth and the sea because the Devil has fallen amongst us. And the Dragon is filled with fury because he knows his time is short."

Hensley stopped, looking at the crowd. No one spoke.

Hensley spoke to the man at the door, "Leinart, can you get me a drink of water? We need some more explaining." He looked at the Fisher sisters and said, "I ain't getting through to you, am I? Am I right? I mean you still don't understand where I'm headed, right?"

"No, sir. We ain't understanding just yet."

Hensley got loud as he told them, "You must have faith that we can get our own back. We can vanquish evil. We can overcome the Oppressor. If you'll watch, I can show you how. If you believe. You must believe I can reveal God's power over evil…if you believe!"

Leinart came back with water, which Hensley downed without hesitation. He handed the empty glass back and turned to the crowd. "What's bothering me is the short time we got left. It's the infernal hurry that's consuming everything at the CEW and the Great Smokey Park and Norris Dam."

Hensley turned to face Mrs. Morrow. "Why?" he asked. "Why did they give you only two weeks to move out of your house? Why did all you all get removed for something you never asked for? Why won't the CEW officials take the time to explain all the commotion they got over there? If they'd just slow down and tell us why they're jerking us around. Just tell us why all those trains are going in with full freight cars, but empty coming back out. If there's somebody at the top who's deciding all this, maybe we ought to do something about that. When it all comes tumbling down, maybe we can go back to the way it used to be before they started taking what's ours."

Hatmaker clapped his hands loudly, which startled everyone. "Yeah," he said. "Go back to how it was. That's what we need. I mean, what's the rush? I can sure understand why the Dragon is filled with fury if they won't tell him nothing, and time's growing short." He looked at everybody, one after the other. "Maybe we need our own Dragon to make them tell us what we want to know. They need to listen to us for a change."

The Fishers nodded. "That's right. You're sure as hell right."

Hensley removed the lid to the box and reached inside, seemingly without a care in the world, pulling out a copperhead as thick as his arm nearly five feet long, curling and writhing around his arm. Hensley gripped the snake directly behind its head, its mouth gaping open, showing slender white fangs and a forked tongue flicking in and out, tasting the air. "Here, Big Man! You! General Groves! I'm talking to you, Boss Man," he yelled, lifting the snake over his head. "I got something for you!"

He looked straight at the sisters. "The serpent cannot hurt you if you believe."

Hatmaker slid away to another chair, and the Fisher sisters huddled together.

Hensley screamed, "Behold!"

Bashie felt her heart in her throat as the serpent's embrace moved down his arm and around his chest.

Half Moon Road

When Hensley made the offertory prayer, Theo translated all the homilies into appeals specifically dedicated to Bashie's recovery. He had closed his eyes, clasping his hands on his lap, trying to will the prayers into his wife, body and soul, such that she would end her long downward slide, somehow regaining her health. Surely, some of what ailed her was grief for their lost baby, but there was some that was just malignancy unrelated to what had been lost. She had been slight of build, slender and graceful before the baby, and he had teased her as lighthearted as possible as the pregnancy progressed about gaining weight in her midsection and the swelling around her ankles and wrists, even her fingers. And he liked to lay a hand lightly on her middle where she had "swallered a watermelon." Sometimes he laid his head onto her abdomen to eavesdrop on the child growing there. Later he thought maybe it had been wrong to tease that way.

Now here we are mid-May, 1944, at the *Foot of the Cross* again he whispered to himself, "Dear God, help Bashie and me best way you see fit. Forgive us our sins. Sustain my beloved wife. Heal her broken heart, if that's what still ails her. Or heal her damaged spirit, her sickness of the soul. Free her from suffering, which will surely free me from same."

All that mattered was for Bashie to be whole again. He thought about her as he departed the church and drove home. Theo had suggested she see the doctor ahead of her next scheduled treatment, but she preferred what she called her "yarbs," saying, "Bring me pokeberry root. And juniper berries if you can find some."

"What will you do with all that?"

"Juniper protects against consumption, and that could be what's wrong with me. Pokeberry root gets boiled, and with honey and ginger it purifies the blood. I'll try some honey with bean flowers to fix me some kind of tea to protect against cancer."

"Cancer?" he gasped. "Do we think what you got's some kind of cancer?"

She chuckled at that. "No, silly. I'm protecting against it. As worn down as I am, I think that's a good idea."

"You're right, you're right," he said, able to breathe again.

She put a hand on his arm. "And violets," she said. "If you find any violets still blooming, pick them for me. That's another tea I can make from little flowers. And Mrs. Delap said to add cayenne to anything and everything. She says it's a cure-all, if you know how to mix it."

Bashie had met Ida Rose Delap a quarter mile outside Elza Gate at the Farmer's Market held in the Woodson Grocery's parking lot where they both shopped twice a month. Mrs. Delap was a plain country women, usually dressed in dungarees under her worn brown skirt, which added to her practical, homespun look. Her face was craggy, lined with wrinkles, especially at her neck and around her green eyes. Her long hair was more gray than dark brown. When Bashie had first met her and said, "Your outfit must be awful hot," the woman had cackled. She'd said, "Well, hit sure is hot," pulling a rebellious strand of hair back behind her ear so it disappeared under her broad-brimmed straw hat. "Vanity requires I hide my very close veins. If you saw my legs without trousers, you'd swear I's a walking road map. Blue lines all going this way 'n' that. I jest keep my lower half all covered up. They's nothing else to be done."

One thing led to another there among the tomatoes and squash, and they sorted through string beans and okra with Bashie somehow connecting with and opening up to this woman, telling how she was searching for ways to relieve herself. Ways to deal with feeling poorly day after day.

Ida Rose picked up a handful of beans, asking, "Have you took any natural medicines?"

Bashie dropped beans back into the bin, answering, "I don't believe so, no. I'm seeing a Dr. Clark over at the new hospital on the Reservation, but I don't know. I'm not feeling well. Not all the time. Do you know about natural medicines, Miz Delap? Is that why you're talking about?"

"Sure do. I know yarbs," she said. "Call me Ida Rose, will you? Hit's my preference." Smiling, which showed poor teeth, she added, "I think you and me, we's going to be friendly." And that was what led Bashie to get Theo picking wildflowers and pokeberry root and such. And how they started stocking up on honey and ginger and cayenne. Also caraway seed.

Ida Rose showed Bashie how to grind the caraway, ginger, and salt, mixing that concoction into butter, so you could eat it like plain bread-and-butter. Sahe told Bashie, "This keeps the hysterics off you."

Bashie took a deep breath. "I got everything else known to man so I don't need them hysterics."

Ida Rose agreed. "Natural cures is a lot better than other things they do to rid a gal of hysterics. I mean, they might hose you down with cold water for an hour, or they might give you some kind of body message."

"What?"

"You know, somebody rubs on you for a while. Ain't that what they call giving a message?"

"Massage. I think that's how you say it."

Ida Rose grinned. "You got it. That's it." And she slapped her knee, laughing heartily. Theo likened the sound she made as so sincere and unselfconscious that he could not hear it without chuckling himself. Thinking back as he sat at church, he recalled how Ida Rose's laughter had not only affected him, but it affected Bashie, who gained a bit of a glow while Ida Rose was there with them.

At the Farmer's Market they were saying their farewells when Ida Rose asked, "You going to be back next time they do Farmer's Market?"

"Of course," Bashie said.

"Well, I'll see you then," Ida Rose said, lifting the bag of squash and cucumbers she'd purchased, turning for the road.

"Wait, Ida Rose. Wait," Bashie said, holding up a hand. "How are you getting home?"

"Same way I always do. Walking."

Theo asked, "Where exactly is home for you?"

"Frost Bottom."

Bashie looked quickly to Theo. "That must be five or six miles from here."

Ida Rose set her bag down, removed her straw hat, and wiped sweat from her brow and temple. "Yup, that sounds about right. I might as well git moving. In a minute or two after I rest up a bit." She put her hat back on, adding, "Don't feel like it's gitting any cooler."

Bashie laughed and clapped her hands. "I believe you're right about us becoming friends. Real good friends. Next time I'll come see you, so tell us where your place is at."

Ida Rose took her hat off again, using it to fan herself. "Well, that sounds fine. I can see you here at the Farmer's Markets, and you can come see me otherwise. I live on Half Moon Road the other side of Walden Ridge. I got a path up across Walden down into

Frost Bottom. That's how come I say it's five or six miles. If you go by car, you got to foller the roads down into Oliver Springs then back to Frost Bottom. More like eleven miles probably. But it's more level. Easier for this old woman to walk."

All through Ida Rose's telling where she lived Bashie was staring at Theo, and he knew what she would say before she said it. "Listen, Ida Rose, Theo and me will drive you home in our car. Save you all that walking and what? Three hours? Four?"

Ida Rose stared at them for a long moment before turning to look behind her. She removed her hat, exhaling a long breath. "That would be awful nice, but I don't want to keep you from what you all need to be doing yourself."

"No trouble," Theo said, knowing that's what Bashie wanted. And after Miz Delap understood it really was all right he went out to the car and came back to pick them up. The women sat in the back seat talking like long lost friends reunited after years apart. The old woman did some explaining about yarbs she was familiar with. Some she had trouble finding. How to prepare some. And some she had never used, but wanted to try out. Bashie mostly listened, and Theo listened, too, all the way to Half Moon Road, not weighing their words, but relishing the sounds they made. The happy sound of Bashie's voice.

"Thay's a old, rusted tractor in my front yard," Ida Rose said. "So you turn in right there."

Theo studied the road and eventually found the turn-in, pulling into a small, weed-stricken yard in front of a weathered, unpainted clapboard house. One story. No front porch. Just a cinder block for a step-up to the front door. He turned off the ignition, and the women were still talking. The windows were down, allowing a light breeze to reach all three of them, but after a few minutes Theo got out to find more of the cooling breeze. While they talked he wandered around the side of the house to see a row of blue iris in profusion. In back a clothes line and a well-worn path to a privy. Around the other side of the house a dilapidated dog house. No sign of a dog.

When he returned to the car, Ida Rose had gotten out with her bag, hat in hand, expressing gratitude to Bashie. "I hope I ain't put you back too far spending all this time bringing me home."

Theo answered before Bashie could. "Miz Delap, I can tell you for a fact that spending time with you is the best possible thing for my wife. Look at her," he said. "All this has been good for her."

Bashie's face turned red. She nodded. "I believe he's right, Ida Rose. It's been good for me, so I hope you don't think I'm selfish saying we'll be back to see you next Friday. If you'll have us, that is."

"I don't have a very big place here," Ida Rose told them, "but you're welcome to come visit any time."

Bashie looked to Theo, who looked right back at her. "I know the way to get here now."

Ida Rose put down her bag and said, "Come here, child," holding out her arms. Bashie moved quickly into the old woman's arms, smiling over her shoulder at her husband. The first smile he hadn't had to coax out of her in weeks.

After they got home, they went about going to be, and later once they were settled in bed Bashie told him, "I like Ida Rose."

"I know you do," he said. "Do you really want to do all the natural stuff she's talking about?" "Might as well," she answered as she snuggled her head under his chin. "Nothing else has worked very long."

He heard a catch in her voice, wondering, *Is it worth following up on this? It's late. She must be tired.*

"My fingers are tingling," she said, and for a moment he thought she was flirting with him in the dark, but she ended that idea when she put a hand on his chest and said, "I can feel you with the palm of this hand, husband. But not with the tips of these fingers."

He reached quickly for her hand. "Oh," he said. "I didn't know. How long have you been like this?"

"Just since you turned out the lights," she said. "I thought I was going crazy for a while. Dr. Clark has told me this could happen. He said it didn't have to happen…but it has."

She wriggled her hand out of his and drew circles on his chest with a finger. "I can't hardly feel you this way, Theo. I know what I'm doing, but I can't hardly feel a tall."

"I'm right here with you," he told her. "We're together no matter what."

They lay quietly for a while without finding sleep. Finally, he said, "You want me to fix you some of that caraway seed mix? I heard Miz Delap say how it's done."

"That can wait until morning, husband. I just want you to hold me like you're doing. Hold me a bit longer, please."

"I'll hold you all night long, darling."

"I know," she whispered. "I know you will."

The Absolute Worst

They were in Hubbell's conference room on the second floor of the Castle, and Buckley tried one last time, asking the Lieutenant, "Bobby, tell me about this Gadget thingamajig."

Blankenship replied, "If I knew anything, I couldn't tell you. No use asking about it. Just let it go."

"That's never going to happen," Buckley said. "And it pisses me off, you saying that. Nobody knows what the Gadget is. That's what they say. But everybody whispers about it when they think the Undercover Man ain't around. Me, I want to know a hell of a lot more than what's being whispered, and I don't care who knows it. Everybody knows we got the Japs on the run. I'm expecting this War won't last another six months. It won't get us into 1946. Mark my words, Bobby. You know I'm right. I want to know about the Gadget. How it's going to beat the Japs."

Blankenship sat down across the table. "Talking like that will get you discharged. I won't be able to help you if there are charges against you for espionage."

"Ess pee what?"

Blankenship looked Buckley right in the eye. "Seriously. Don't be asking around about the Gadget. General Groves will kick you right off the Reservation if he finds out how curious you are. Today we've got something else to discuss. A report from one of our agents. About a recent secret meeting."

"I'm listening."

"Before I read this," he said, waving a paper at Buckley, "let me ask, do you know anything about a Dragon over in Clinton?"

"Nope. Never heard of no Clinton Dragon. Why do you want to know?"

"Our agent believes the group that was being surveilled last week is planning sabotage somewhere on the CEW Reservation. Or perhaps an attack on an administrator or scientist."

"What exactly is sabotage?" Buckley said. "And 'Sir Vailed.' Who's he?"

"Being watched closely. That's what surveilled means. And sabotage is any act that damages equipment or facilities."

"Fay silly tees?'

"Facilities means buildings. Sabotage can result from wrecking equipment. From fires, explosions, destructive acts of any sort. That's sabotage." He placed the paper on the table and began reading. "It says here the agent attended a church meeting nine days ago when a man did some snake handling."

"So?" Buckley said. "I seen snake handling afore. Damn fool preachers will do about anything to get a collection plate going around. What did your agent think about the serpents? Bet he never seen a grown man playing with serpents like they do. Was that in the report?"

Blankenship admitted, "The agent was duly impressed with the snake. But it was what was said during the meeting that interests us. The preacher told a story about the book of Revelations. Something about a Dragon. The general impression I get from reading the entire report is that the preacher contends that Dragon is Satan. This apparently confused our agent who reported that, 'The preacher described the Dragon as fighting evil. The way the preacher, Hensley, told his story, the Dragon wasn't the Devil. The Dragon opposed evil, and the current manifestation of evil is us here at the CEW.' The logic is shaky, but the conclusion is clear. The Clinton Engineer Works is in jeopardy as far as these folks are concerned. They see us as evil."

Buckley leaned back in his chair, crossing his legs at the ankles. "Who's your agent?"

"You don't need to know that," Blankenship said. "You merely need to know what was reported."

Buckley rubbed his face. "You're probably right this time, but stop saying that, will you? Stop telling me I don't need to know something. You don't know what I need to know. I'm the onliest one that knows that. If something flustrates me, it affects my feel for what's going on. You don't want that. You want me free-wheeling my way through things."

Now Blankenship pushed back from the table. "I hear you. I'll take that into consideration. How do you see this Dragon versus evil concept? Revelations has the angels defeating the Dragon, yet this Hensley fellow made a big to-do about needing a Dragon to oppose the CEW. Captain Hubbell and I have reviewed this report, focusing on a quote the agent emphasized: 'The Dragon needs to *take down* a giant.' *Take down* translates to *kill*. And that led us to compiling a list of key officials and scientists. Sabotage could mean destruction of equipment and facilities, but it could also mean assassination of CEW leaders. We've got to be aware of both possibilities."

"Tell me the preacher's name again. His whole name."

Blankenship smiled. "That's something you do need to know. He's George Hensley."

Buckley smiled, too. "The guy from Chattanooga. Yeah, I heard of him." He rubbed his nose. "Now you got something else for me. Let's have it."

"As a matter of fact, I do. How'd you know that?"

"From the way you been acting. Like you had something special to tell me. But what you've already said wadn exactly special, not that I could see."

Blankenship reached behind to the desk and retrieved a manila folder. "I wish I knew how you do it."

"I pay attention to things," Buckley said. "Watch close, and I'll teach you a thing or two. Now what you been holding back? Let's have it."

"Our agent reported that Hensley was bitten by a snake. On the hand in the flesh between forefinger and thumb. However, the bite didn't seem to affect him."

"Maybe not then," Buckley said. "But I bet his hand turned black within six hours. And I'd bet you a hunnert dollars he's been laid low."

"You speaking from experience?"

"Yup. I had experience with snakes. Copperheads mostly. First time I got bit I thought I was a goner. Drank whiskey four days straight. Hand swole up. Turned mottled purple and yellow. Then black. I drank like they's no tomorrow. But tomorrow came, didn't it? A whole slew of tomorrows."

Blankenship studied the report a while, and Buckley lit a cigarette. He rose from the table and paced around the room, stopping now and then to look out the windows and listen to the dozers at work gouging roadways on the ridge. There was more dirt than green out the way he was looking. More rocky debris than grass and leaves. Without any recent rain the dozers were enshrouded in clouds of dust swirling in the breeze. Blankenship noticed Buckley's gaze and said, "I hear they're putting in a new road or street every day. They're putting those flat-top houses made of cemesto at the rate of thirty-five per day, seven days a week."

"Never heard of this cemesto stuff," Buckley said. "But they's sure a whole hell of a lot going on. This place is like nowhere else I ever been. Craziest damn bidness I ever seen." He turned to Blankenship and discovered he wasn't listening, just reading the folder.

Finally, Blankenship noticed he was being watched. "I don't know. This might not be right. This Dragon business might turn out to be a wild goose chase. We don't have much to go on. What I've been reading here," and he tapped the folder "is a preliminary list of key personnel we'd need to safeguard."

"How many names on the list?"

"182. And they're all spread out over the CEW. Most at Y-12. Fewer at X-10 and K-25, but we have quite a few here at the Castle."

"So it's not going to be easy to keep em safe, is it?"

"No, it won't be easy," Blankenship agreed. "And I'm not even counting the ones that move between and among the respective plants. And sites outside Tennessee. They don't sit still, and that merely adds to our paranoia."

Buckley's brow wrinkled. "Pair of what?"

"Paranoia. That means thinking somebody's out to get you even if nobody really is."

"Huh. Sounds like a good way to operate, if you ast me."

Blankenship grabbed a notepad and scribbled a few words. "Making sure I remember what you said," he explained. "Sometimes you say something I hadn't considered, and I want to recall it later so I can go over it again when you're not around."

"That makes a difference?" Buckley asked. "If I'm not there?"

"You're distracting sometimes," Blankenship said. "I don't want to miss anything you might say next. If I concentrate on one thing, I could miss the next thing. That's why I write it down. For later." He stared at his notes. "Want to see this?"

"Naw. I don't read so fast as you do."

"Yeah. I figured reading's not your hobby. But that's intriguing, too. How you can get around here without reading."

Buckley stared back out the window. "If you pay close attention, people will tell you more by the way they behave than by what printed words will tell." He returned to the table and said, "Let's go at this Dragon story again from a new direction. Say that there is a Dragon out there, and he's going to try to do some serious damage. And what's worse, that he's going to come after somebody real important. What's the most important building that's going up here? Who's the most important soldier here? The most important scientist?"

For a moment Blankenship remained silent. Then he said, "Hard to say what's the most important building. They're building everywhere. If I had to pick a place to protect most, it would be here. The Castle on the Hill. If this place blew up, we'd lose generals and subordinate officers. Records. Communication equipment. Support staff. You name it."

"Who do we start with?"

"Groves. He's personally involved in everything everywhere. The man's a human dynamo. Nothing happens without his say-so."

"What if he ain't around any more? What happens?"

"They'll replace him," Blankenship said. "They'll have to. But it would take a while for his replacement to get up-to-speed. And I'm just talking about here in Tennessee. His replacement would need to do the same thing in New York, Chicago, Washington State, New Mexico. And Washington, D.C."

"Good God!"

"The entire Manhattan Project would come to a halt," Blankenship said. "The War Effort would be hamstrung. And the operation is huge. I cannot really describe how much money is involved in getting things done here. And getting them done as quickly as possible. That's necessary to save American lives all around the world."

"I get it," Buckley said. "If Groves is gone, and I mean gone forever, as in D. E. D. …dead…then you slow this place to a crawl for a year, maybe fifteen months. Is that right? And you do the same in them other places? And we still win the war, but it takes a few more years."

"And more lives," Blankenship said. "But I don't know. I'm not sure if all the sites would shut down. Maybe they would. But how can they? Groves says everything that's going on here is critical for the War Effort. I expect he's singing that same tune everywhere he goes. The man's a dynamic leader, that's for sure. Without him, things would get stalled."

Buckley said, "Will Groves' replacement be as good as him?"

Blankenship didn't answer.

Buckley said, "That's how we need to go along like there's a Clinton Dragon, and he's coming after Groves. Because, if Groves gets his ass killed off, it might just lose the war. Somebody's trying to kill him to make that happen. Is that what you're saying?"

Blankenship nodded. "That's the worst that could happen."

Buckley nodded, too, saying, "That's what you got to get ready for. The worst that could happen. That's our job, Bobby. Stopping the worst."

"You ready?"

Buckley took a long drag on his cigarette, blowing a plume of smoke overhead and grinning. Then he said, "Oh, hell, yeah. I'm familiar with the absolute worst there is. I can handle it."

Roads and Streets

Years later he will recall, *There was a War on, so standards were never exactly fixed in place. Nothing lasted very long.* Sgt. Marcus Brummett will also remember he had gone about as far as a slender branch of guesswork could take him. Way out there on a limb.

*****

And it comes back to him moment to moment very much like this:

He's got to go slow and careful because of the pain lingering down his right leg. It's acting up today, but he's dealing with it. He's done his stretching. Done some limbering up in the parking lot before he got to the car, so it's a little better now. Barely tolerable. In most cases a problem like his will kick you out of the Army, but he's learned to hide pain.

As he turns off California Avenue onto Outer Drive he's searching for connections between all the new roads, avenues, lanes, and streets. You name it, he needs to know it like the back of his hand. His job depends on getting where he needs to go without backtracking or wasting time. And wouldn't it be nice if things didn't change so much every day? He's learned the hard way they can put in a new road every damn day, which can screw you up royally.

But by August, 1943 Outer Drive is laid out really well. Through the trees atop the ridge he glimpses the Cumberland Plateau, a mountain range fifty miles to the west, although not so well-known as the Great Smokies, an equal distance to the east. California has taken him north from the Turnpike. Outer Drive takes him southwest. He's pleased to have this much straight, marked out clearly in his mind's eye.

His commanding officer, General Leslie Groves, has Marcus drive him everywhere around this bustling 56,000 acre complex known as Clinton Engineer Works, a sprawling Federal District still under construction along the valleys and ridges in this rural section of East Tennessee. The CEW has over twenty thousand "construction soldiers" struggling to fulfill Groves' ambitions for winning the War. Everybody has questions about what's going on, but The Man is fond of saying, "You'll be informed when it's time for you to know."

Seven months ago Marcus had back-to-back episodes with his sciatica, and he thought if Groves noticed, that would be the end of Brummett, the driver.

He might even get put on disability, out of it all. Not ready for that. Not by a damned sight! He understood right from the start it would be a primo assignment, but also no picnic. You'd be judged every second, and if you didn't satisfy the General, you'd be subject to a quick trip out the door. Out of the CEW.

But being assigned to The Man has its perks: Marcus drives a brand new Ford coupe, a dark, unmarked vehicle kept spit polish clean, which means he's getting it washed nearly every other day to keep the red mud off it. Monthly tune-ups. Groves could be here a week or ten days or merely a single day, and then, before you know it, he's gone. Marcus will get a call at his quarters at the Guest House, a gray, two-story building set halfway up one of the ridges, where the VIP's stay. Marcus is supposed to call to check in with the front desk every six hours or so. The phone service at the CEW is going through its own growing pains, so most of the time a guy at the front desk has messages for him. Often tells him to collect Groves at the Knoxville train station in an hour. So he's off again like Snider's pup, trying to keep the hip and back loose.

The War against Germany and Japan's been dragging on a year and a half. Except for German surrender in Stalingrad back in January, nothing much to celebrate, that's for sure. And around here the CEW is altered daily with great swaths of rural woodland cut down and bulldozed so roads can be laid out, and all manner of buildings go up. Houses, shops, dormitories, factories, warehouses, assorted industrial structures spring up every day in the intense summer heat and humidity. But street and road signage hasn't kept up, and most of it is gravel and mud or sometimes rough blacktop. You just have to know where you need to go, where to turn, how to get back where you came from. Things are changing faster than anybody's ready for.

Nights are a different story. When he drops Groves off around 1800 hours, Marcus is free to do as he wants, and he's fallen hard for a slender little sandy-haired girl down at the Central Bus Terminal Cafe. She's only been there a couple of weeks, but he's got himself almost convinced she's in love with him. She knows about his sciatica. When she gets a break from waiting tables, she walks with him around the Terminal. She can see if his pain is letting up. Sometimes he'd rather just sit at the counter, but she gets him up to walk around, and it almost always drives the pain away. Everything about her, even the faint down on her cheek, brings a quiet soaring in his heart. She's not beautiful in a conventional way, but she's a compelling armful. She's smitten him. He's got skylark energy whenever he thinks about her.

Her name's Dorothy Swicegood, and she's got this good friend who works beside her at the Café, a short, sturdy dark-haired girl named Carlotta Albertini from New Jersey. Carlotta's funny and smart. Older than Dorothy, she calls her friend Dot, so Marcus calls her Dot too. It's like Carlotta's her older sister or cousin watching over Dot, not letting any guys, soldiers, construction workers, or anybody else give her any grief as she's waiting tables. Dot's always whispering and sniggering with Carlotta, and Marcus has this feeling sometimes their sniggering's about him. But in a good way. Carlotta knows why Dot walks with him, but she keeps it quiet. Marcus never catches Dot off guard. She catches him. He can't help feeling something in his heart has caught and turned over because of Dot Swicegood. She could be for keeps, and surely Carlotta is aware of how he feels. He'd like to get her help with Dot, but maybe not just yet. Trying to work it out on his own. And stretching and walking around the parking lot to keep limber.

He's held off talking about Dot with any of his buddies. Eddie's one of the guys from down at the Motor Pool. Good looking guy. Like Dana Andrews, but he's narrow-shouldered. Carlotta's said Dot dated Eddie a couple of times before Marcus came on the scene. Nothing going on between them now. She doesn't think there is.

Marcus has mixed feelings about some of the guys that come in. He likes acting the fool with some of the bus drivers who get rowdy now and then. But mostly, Marcus hangs out with a guy named Reggie, another named Ernest, both pretty wild characters; he learns about short cuts from them and about dead-end roads. They're not rocket scientists, but they know the roads.

Eddie talks about the women up in Happy Valley. "They just give it away, if you keep on trying," he says. "You got to sweet talk them." Marcus hasn't been in Happy Valley much. That's where K-25 is. Might be a good idea to explore Happy Valley someday.

One morning Dot's not at the Café, so Carlotta's center stage. She brings him eggs, grits, and biscuits, surprising him as she sets down the plate. "So, Marcus, you're driving for one of the Big Shots, right?" She's seen the car he drives, which is just a dark blue color, but first class in quality so there's no denying his passenger is high ranking. He stops trying to evade her questions, but keeps Groves' name out of it. Still, she's figured out he's connected with the Brass somehow. She whispers, "See that officer in the corner back there, talking with the baldheaded guy? He's in charge of the *Oak Ridge Journal.*"

"What?"

She wipes a spot off the counter. "The baldheaded guy runs the newspaper over in Clinton. Can't remember his name...Williams or Walker. Something with a W. Anyway, he loves nothing better than to do a big, sensational story on things related to the War. I know you drive the Brass, but you don't let on about it, so I'm figuring it wouldn't be good for you to become newsworthy." She's serious about this, looking out for him.

But Carlotta's called into the kitchen letting him focus on something else. He doesn't know enough about Dot. She has three younger brothers back home on the farm outside the little town of Sweetwater, Tennessee, 75 miles south. She worked at Y-12 a while.

He's mulling that over when somebody taps him on the shoulder. It's the baldheaded character. "Mind if I sit down?" Marcus shrugs, studying the man.

Marcus is wary. "What can I do for you?"

"My name's Horace Wells. Run the paper over in Clinton. I've seen you here before."

"Food's good here."

Wells starts talking about how they're putting up so many new houses every day, "flattops" he calls them, made out of concrete and asbestos, which is known as cemesto. And he's right about that. The little box-shaped houses are going up everywhere. Eventually, the guy runs out of small talk. Finally getting down to brass tacks.

He says, "I've heard you're driver for a VIP. One of the generals here. Is that right?"

"Where'd you hear that?"

"Won't divulge my sources."

Is this a trap of some kind? Some kind of test? That's how Marcus sees it. Groves might have sent this newspaper guy to interrogate him. *Got to be careful here.*

"If you were driving an officer around," Wells says, "would you be driving that shiny new Ford out front?"

"Why do you think that?" he says.

The guy gets testy. "You didn't exactly answer yes or no, did you?"

"Who pointed you in my direction anyway?" Marcus digs at him a little bit. "Was it some female did it?" That would be good to know.

"I didn't say it was a woman, did I?"

"Sounds like someone doesn't know what they're talking about."

The man gets friendly, smiling what seems honest. "The person who pointed you out I won't identify. Last month I lost a good reporter. Fellow got banned from the CEW. He was hot on the trail of something big. An important story. There's been a surge of CEW employees getting sick, and people need to be informed about whatever's causing it. But nobody's talking about it. Somebody high up decided against that. We were trying to tell people about some kind of sickness, something like a plague running rampant through the dorms and the trailer parks. Not necessarily fatal, but serious enough as is."

Marcus scratches his jaw. "You said, 'person' so I figure it's probably a female. You're just fishing for information. Which I can't give you."

The guy pushes away from the counter. "Fishing you say. Well, I suppose I might have hooked a big one, too. That's the way it looks. I've seen some of the afflictions…guys with fevers, hair falling out, bleeding at the gums, their white blood cell count soaring. Something insidious is hurting men employed in the CEW. Maybe even killing some of them." He studies Marcus, deciding if more detail is necessary. Decides against it. "But you're not talking, right? At least, not yet. I'm hoping to change your mind somehow. Whatever it is, prompt corrective measures need to be taken." Marcus sees the determination in his face. "Good afternoon, Sergeant. I hope to talk with you again sometime."

Marcus's daily pilgrimages around the CEW are wandering affairs. Last week Groves was in town Monday through Saturday, and Marcus was obliged to break two dates with Dot, which left her understandably perturbed. So he's got to make it up to her, or she might just go find some other guy. She wouldn't have to look long. 19-year-old Miss Dot Swicegood is pure perfection, soft and smooth everywhere that counts. A year out of high school, she's seven years his junior, a small-town girl. She's a little unpredictable, a little unruly, which has allure of its own. Not something you read in books or see in the movies. All he knows is whenever she takes his order at the café, he's got the impulse to reach out and touch her to see if she's real.

He goes out scouting roads and streets and learns Virginia Avenue but gets lost a couple minutes on Hillside Road. He keeps going and is able to map out Illinois Avenue, Jefferson Avenue, and finally Robertsville Road. So he's starting to feel pretty good about all this, wondering when Groves will want to run through those places. Groves likes to see everything with his own eyes, which makes sense if you're the General. If you're his driver, not so much.

A large barrel-chested man with a gray brush moustache, Groves is no-nonsense. Has a direct approach about things. He'll tell Marcus, "Take me to X-10." (Way down Bethel Valley Road). Or "Take me to Y-12." (Scarboro Road down to Bear Creek Road). You can't even get close to those mammoth structures without a high priority pass, which, of course, Groves uses. Hordes of men and machines working day and night to build more of everything. Rows of debris, long lines of mangled trees and brush pushed into piles are burning in place instead of being hauled away. There's swirling smoke and cinders as well as a constant humming and high-speed buzzing all through the valley.

Dot has complained about how the CEW seems so chaotic, not like home. She's grumbling, "Things are different here. Almost all the people in the CEW are from somewhere else. And there's people working a while. Then they quit, even though wages here are far better than anywhere else. Or they're fired. The bosses want product, product, product. There's precious little said about workers' health or safety. This place is crazy! That's why I left Y-12 and came here to help Carlotta."

It's Carlotta who tells him Dot sends most of her paycheck home to Sweetwater every two weeks. He sees her as one of those heart of gold types. Part of her wild and undeniably luscious. Another part of her family-oriented and protective.

He says, "Yeah, not very many people even knew this whole area existed before the War. I believe the CEW will settle down. You watch, we'll see things for the better, not worse." A smile softens her mouth just a little, and she looks so pretty. If she was a little taller, she might be another Ingrid Bergman. When he watches her, he feels like he's been dipped in magic waters. Bathed clean.

Unlike Dot, the General doesn't make friends. He treats everyone the same way---scientists, administrators, contractors, and, of course, his driver. He tells you what he wants, holds you accountable, no slack given. And you got to see the world the way he tells you to see it. On the other hand, Dot...well, she's downright puzzling. She's usually good, seeming content. Mellow, you might say. But there's also a couple of times when she's sarcastic. Sullen. Bitter somehow for no good reason.

Marcus studies Groves' every move, every decision, every utterance. He isn't exactly fond of Groves, but he delights in the driving, especially when Groves is out of town. Oh, he's obligated to transport the occasional VIP while The Man's gone, but Groves can show up without much notice, so Marcus is mostly exempt from taxi duty. But when he knows Groves is out of state for a while…usually the West Coast or New York City…Marcus can make good money hauling folks to the Plantation Club in Harriman or the Ritz Club in Clinton. He gets a lot of jobs by calling the Guest House. Driving officers to nightclubs, that's when his mind is freed up, given pause to stray and roam, unafraid to take a wrong turn or backtrack if need be. He need not account for gasoline nor milage on the coupe. It's all free and clear. Of course, that could change. Everything's changing. And there's some few times when what's changed one day changes back the next, faster than you can say Jack Robinson. And the trains arriving all day long, all of them loaded full to bursting with equipment, material, supplies and more and more men coming in. Truck convoys, too, all heavy laden with equipment or tools or food. Everything's going in. Nothing's coming out.

But, as well as he's doing, when he thinks about Dot, Marcus Brummett lacks a confident heart. He's no Clark Gable, unlikely to sweep a girl off her feet. He's more like Jimmy Stewart, gangly, skinny, easy to talk to. That's how he sees himself. Not exactly Mr. Smith Goes to Washington. Just your regular guy.

Some big shot up north has sent three large boxes of chocolate bars to The Man. A blatant attempt to get on Groves' good side, but it doesn't work because Groves prefers rock candy, and he says, "Brummett, keep these chocolates safe. We might give them to somebody coming to the Guest House next Thursday. Special guests from New Mexico." But the special guests never show, and finally Groves says, "Put the candy to good use, Sergeant. I don't need the details. Just take care of it." While the General's reading in the back seat Marcus is reaching for the sweet stuff beside him in the front seat, pulling it closer.

So one night after her shift Marcus drives Dot to Clinton, eight miles east if you follow Highway 61 along the Clinch River. At 2100 hours the town's asleep. He parks the car in the deserted high school parking lot. Without explanation, he hands her two Hershey bars. She tastes them, wiping at a drip off her lower lip. She nearly has a fit of ecstasy. "Oooh," she murmurs. "This is….oooh!" Her smile brightens up the night, and her kiss is tinged with milk chocolate.

Later back at the CEW they're able to get into one of the late dances at Grove Center tennis courts, and even as balmy and muggy as it is, Dot's very, very grateful. He thinks maybe she's more than merely grateful. Maybe willing to do more than hold hands.

After the walk back to the coupe he slides in behind the wheel as she moves across the bench seat until her thigh brushes his. Without thinking he pulls her even closer, and things start going the way he'd been hoping they would. She has a new voice that comes deep down in her throat, and he's not processing her words so much as taking in her whispers and moans. Both out of breath, their mouths hungry to be one with each other.

He coaxes her, drawing her to the backseat where they go a little further. He wants her to bring him all she's got, but too soon he feels her bristle slightly, which is enough to burst the bubble around his heart.

She backs away a few inches, whispering, "I'm sorry."

He's misjudged her. "It's all right," he says. "Forget it." But he sure as hell won't forget.

Even so, he has a rush of true feeling. The head-over-heels kind. Whenever she's within arm's reach it's like that. He wants her, and sometimes she might feel the same way. There are snippets coming from the loud speaker 200 yards away back on the tennis courts: a voice drifting through the dark humidity, Nat King Cole's *It's Only a Paper Moon.* She pushes the door open, standing there. "Let's just dance one last dance."

She molds her figure into his, her face snug under his chin. They're swaying to the music without moving their feet. Eventually, they come up for air again. Dot steps away, silhouetted against the debris fires illuminating the northern ridge, turning to him. "You've got hungry hands." She examines his face, smiling and adding, "I'm not complaining. That's just how you are."

He says, "Are you saying that's okay?"

She nods. "Every now and then it is," she says, reaching over to tap his belt buckle. "I'll let you know when it's not." His blood quickens, and he wonders if she feels it, too. He can't believe she's giving him what he's already got. He's anxious about losing that. Losing her. Abject at the thought of it.

He drops her off at the Café. It's good the place is open seven days a week, all 24 hours. Immediately, she gravitates to Carlotta who's in charge again. He drives slowly back to the Guest house, his mind wandering. Later he dreams about her wriggling and moaning in his arms, breathing in his ear. He can feel her, but she's nowhere in sight.

The next morning Groves is in town. He stays three days, keeping Marcus on his toes all the while. This time after Groves departs Marcus starts a regular routine of scouting out the entire District, but he gets irritated at the prospect of merely wandering all around, trying to stay well-informed about existing roads and those which will soon exist. Each day he discovers another new road, which upsets his picture of the entire CEW. Out of a sense of frustration he decides to go straight to the source. That is, the Roads and Streets

Office. He's thinking *Somebody has got to be planning where the roads will go. It's not random. Can't be.*

At Roads and Streets he has a real lucky stroke involving a dowdy looking secretary who. he's guessing isn't used to sweet talk. She must be good at her job, but frumpy, too heavy, using no make-up when she really should. Badly chewed fingernails. No nail polish. H e asks for a list of new streets, but she scorns him. "We don't copy lists for just anybody that asks," and she turns away. That's that.

Marcus asks someone else. But the other clerks defer to the woman…her name's Moynihan…and Marcus thinks maybe he's struck out. Yet he scouts around a bit more, learning other offices are more welcoming than Moynihan's, some sporting vases of flowers, some photos of spouses, children, and such. Moynihan's office is destitute of anything personal, and they don't have a fan, so it's too warm, too sticky around Moynihan.

So he thinks things over, decides to risk trying something he never thought he'd do, and goes back to Moynihan, summarizing his request again, "I hope you'll give my request more thought. I work for General Groves." He drops that last bit on her, trying not to over-do it. Letting Groves' name do the heavy lifting. Without waiting for a reply, he leaves, coming back with a tin of Hershey. "For you, Miss Moynihan." He adds. "I'm Marcus Brummett," offering his hand. No reaction. None at all. But he has a chance to study her face and body language. She's pretty nice looking underneath all that pudge, and now she's sporting ruddy splotches on her cheeks and neck as she's exiting into an adjacent file room.

"Shoot!" he says under his breath. Backing away from the counter, he's surprised by a tall, athletic woman standing at a desk near the door. She's holds up her hand, lowers her voice.

"She's Abigail Beatrice Moynihan. She signs things that way. I call her Bea, and I know her better than anybody else around here." Marcus doesn't know what to make of all that, but it's like he's known the tall girl for years. He thinks he clicks with her.

"Thank you, ma'am," he says. "I appreciate it. Who are you, if I might ask?"

She shakes her head. "I'm not so important as Miss Moynihan."

"You are to me," he says, smiling his most persuasive smile.

"Trudy Allistair," she says, tapping her sternum. "I was in another office upstairs, but they moved us all out last Monday. I loved that job. Wanted to keep it." Then she looks over her shoulder. "Guess I was lucky to get on here. She's a good boss really. Just not much of a talker, you know?"

"You're a life saver. Couldn't have connected with her without you," he says. When he's outside the building, he stretches down to touch his toes a few seconds. A little tight today, so he walks the circumference of the parking lot, which helps a bit.

Marcus keeps stopping by Roads and Streets with whatever he thinks might soften up the ladies. A pair of nylons during wartime is rare as hen's teeth; he'd had to use Groves' name to finagle them at Miller's Department Store. When he holds them up, Moynihan turns beet red before tugging them out of his hand, retreating into her office. Marcus hands a pair to Trudy. He turns to go, but thinks better of it, turning back to her. "By the way, you like chocolate, don't you?"

Turns out she's crazy for it. Who would have thunk it? So Trudy's warming up more than Moynihan is, and Marcus is wracking his brain trying to determine his next move when Moynihan returns. "If you'll come back tomorrow afternoon", she says nervously, "after 15:30, we'll have something for you." She's not about to say anything else. Trudy's not looking up from her typewriter, but she's grinning at the keys.

He learns Moynihan and Trudy can tell him ten days in advance where streets will be coming in, so Marcus gets to go see for himself. Based on what they tell him, he scribbles on a small notepad, making out a rough approximation of the new street map. He keeps the notes in a pocket so he can add to them any time he needs to. He likes Trudy more than Miss Moynihan, and he realizes he understands them better than he understands Dot.

He's got some idea about what likes. Doesn't like. What she'll do. Won't do. He's pleased with how things have gone so far with Carlotta, Moynihan, and Trudy. Not yet with Dot.

This particular afternoon he drives around most of the CEW, exploring freshly graveled roads and a few new macadamized streets winding through the valleys and ridges. He's more familiar now with Bear Creek Valley and especially Bethel Valley. Over the next month with Moynihan's updates Marcus navigates everywhere he needs to go. He knows the Townsite, Y-12, K-25, X-10, S-50---all that and the various plants and warehouses scattered all through the district. He'd be glad if all the construction, all the new roads, all these changes would just stop right here and now. But the CEW keeps on growing, especially west of Grove Center. The whole place is in flux. People showing up. People quitting, Some getting fired, some just not there anymore.

One day at lunch Carlotta pours a coffee refill, quietly telling him to look across the room at two men at the back table. "Take a good look, but don't be obvious. I'll be back to you." She takes the coffee pot to the other end of the counter and four thirsty bus drivers.

Marcus fakes a yawn, stretching his hands overhead, twisting around to view the whole room, but the men are facing away from him. Can't see their faces. They seem familiar, but how can you really tell?

Carlotta returns, deliberately sloshes some coffee onto the counter, busying herself with a rag. Lowering her voice so no one else can hear, she says, "Ever heard of the Code of Wartime Practices?"

"Nope." He glances back there again.

"The guy with the glasses is Horace Wells, editor of the paper in Clinton. The *Courier.* The officer is Captain Bill Wallace. We see him here regular, four or five times a week. Wells just once a week."

"Okay," Marcus says, unsure what to make of that.

"Those two meet here, mostly gabbing so long their coffee gets cold. I keep the refills coming for them. They're discreet, taking pains to keep anyone from hearing what they're saying, but I guess they trust me. Or maybe they forget I'm there so I hear a few tidbits they're going on about. They don't pay any attention to me, and they argue about the same stuff every time. Secrecy and such. Sometimes talking about weapons…something called atomic energy, whatever that is…something else called Blue Tone or Blue Tone Eyum. Something like that. Sounds Spanish, you know what I mean? Or maybe like Latin. It's this Wartime Practices thing I bet you. And the secrets, all their secrets."

"Wartime Practices?" he says.

She tosses her rag into the sink. "Keep your voice down." She glances back in the corner. "Wells says the

Code of Wartime Practices is just censorship, plain and simple, and he doesn't like censorship one little bit. The military tells editors what they can and can't put in their newspaper, and Wells is fit to be tied. Wallace won't give an inch. That's why they're growling back and forth at each other."

"I hear you."

She studies him a moment, deciding something. "Go somewhere for maybe a half hour. Then come back, and we can talk more. Talk privately."

Deliberately, Marcus shakes his head. "You're not pulling my leg about all this, are you?"

"I'm not," she says. No funny business. "I promise you that."

Marcus drives up to Jackson Square to check the movie marquee. The Ridge Theater's still showing one he's already seen, Jean Tierney and Don Ameche in *Heaven Can Wait*. Twenty minutes later when he's back at the Café Wells and Wallace are gone. There's two high school boys bussing tables, and an older woman he doesn't know, she's taking orders at the counter. Carlotta waves him back to the store room.

She starts with, "You know about Y-12, don't you?"

"I know my boss visits there every week or so, but he has me stay with the car. I know how to get there, which gate to go in, where to park. It's a big, noisy set up. Constant droning racket. Takes a while to get used to it." Then he remembers, "There's light poles all around Y-12 so it's like daytime 24 hours a day, and there's no birds singing now. Seems like they're all gone."

Carlotta's grim, as if doing some kind of calculating. "Yeah, that's Y-12 all right, but you don't know about calutrons? The alpha and the beta?"

"The what?"

She looks around the room. "You don't need to share this with anybody else, okay? This is just between you and me." She looks at the doorway, then back at him. "I hate all the hush-hush around here. I got to get a few things off my chest. Got to tell somebody I trust." She blinks several times. "Y-12 has a whole slew of calutrons. Some are called alpha's, some called beta's. Not sure what makes them different like that. Y-12's where I met Dot you know."

"Didn't know that," he says. "So are calutrons what Wallace and Wells talk about?"

Her smile is bitter. "Don't let anybody hear you asking about calutrons. They might want to know where you heard about them, which could backfire on me. Calutron duty is War-related work. Some of the girls, they had to see the doctors, and a couple had to have blood transfusions. But they weren't doing the calutrons. They worked in the labs."

He says, "You can trust me."

"And Dot can, too, right?" she says. He nods, more interested now that Dot's involved.

"The calutrons are big box-like machines with knobs and dials that need constant adjusting. Instead of getting male technicians to run them, they hire young women like me and Dot to do it. You have to turn a few dials to keep a needle inside a certain zone, and that darn thing's jittery. Gets out of hand if you're not watching close. Most men don't have the patience for it. Dot was real good with those dials. I wasn't bad myself."

He nods. "What's a calutron do? What's it for?"

"I don't really know, and you're not supposed to ask. There's a lot of calutrons, and none of us girls actually knew what we were doing nursing dials. A couple snotty guys we call White Coats come looking over our shoulders, scolding us for not keeping the needles where they need to be. Everything depended on the dials.

"So anyway, Dot finally had enough of the griping and nitpicking. A guy was standing right behind her, and it got on her last nerve. She whirled around, shouting, 'You think you can do better? Do you?' Well, that could have curdled our milk, if you get my drift. Turned out when he tried to show her how to do it he couldn't do as good as she did. In fact, all the White Coats did lousy. Girls like me and Dot did the best, and they couldn't say we didn't! That was how Miss Dot Swicegood got a commendation letter for Quality of Work."

"I didn't know any of this," he says. "She never said anything."

"Course not," she says. "Dot did way better than the White Coats. So they stopped bothering us."

"What's this got to do with me?"

"The dials are one thing, but it's got complicated recently, and knowing certain things can get you in trouble here. I've been worried that Dot might have said too much about the calutrons. Something she ought not talk about. I'm not the problem. I'm extra careful. You're the first person I've talked to about calutrons." She pulls her hair behind one ear. Because she's hesitating he's got a hunch Carlotta's trying to let him down easy.

This. Is. Not. Good.

Carlotta settles into a wooden chair, suddenly looking bushed, lighting a cigarette, smoke drifting overhead. He holds off saying anything, not wanting to push, but it's killing him, waiting like this.

Carlotta says, "I got this Café job before Dot did, and she followed a couple weeks later. We had been at Y-12 doing the calutrons, but Dot got sickly. I didn't see it. Not sure what it was. After that, maybe three days later, I went to see her, and she looked poorly. I asked her what was wrong, what happened? She wouldn't talk about it. I had my own reasons for getting out of Y-12, but it must have been something else for Dot. There's too many darn secrets around here! And it's just worn me down, fretting about it." She looks him direct in his face. "I can't think of what to do about all this. I need help is what I'm saying."

"What do you mean 'she looked poorly?'"

Carlotta freezes, stares out the door, not at him. He asks, "What's the matter? Did I say something wrong?"

She wipes at her eyes. "No, you're all right. Still I'm worried about her. At Y-12 they had us be very, very careful. Very clean. And you know, there had to be a reason for all that. But they never said what it was about. Maybe it wasn't anything. But if it's something, it could be bad. Dangerous. Like they're saying about Wartime Practices."

Her voice is quavering, and it sure seems like a big something to do with Dot. He's on guard about whatever's coming next, trusting Carlotta to tell it straight, not sure he's ready to hear it.

She says, "At Y-12 I wasn't happy to work all shift playing with needles. I wanted to get back into Food Service. I grew up working in my uncle's restaurant, and I can maneuver blindfolded around a kitchen. That's why I'm here. But something else happened with Dot. I can't tell you what it was because I was here, and she was still at Y-12."

"Is she…Is it serious?"

"Don't know," she says. "But she's told me how you two have been getting along, getting closer, and I decided you need to know."

"I don't get you."

"Oh, I think you do," she says with a sharp, sudden look, like she's somehow angry. She's shows a little flint in her eye, which makes him think, *It's like she was there in the backseat with us.* And now she's making him figure it out on his own. He wants to ask again, but

she gets back to work, and he waits around nearly an hour for Dot, who never shows. He asks Carlotta about it. She merely shrugs her shoulders. "Your guess is as good as mine." But his mind is racing, curious and anxious about Dot, worried why Carlotta's brought all this up. Why now?

Eddie and the boys wander in around 1800 hours, and they've already got a buzz on. Ernest, Reggie, Tommy, and a couple of guys Marcus has seen around, but doesn't know their names. The whole bunch is loud, sliding chairs noisily away from the table, laughing about the least little thing. Nothing funny to anyone else. A couple sitting near them gets up and moves to a booth across the room. Eddie saunters to the counter right next to Marcus. The odor of beer arrives with him. "Wonder what's got into those two," he mutters, leering in the couple's direction.

"Where you guys been?" Marcus says. "Seems like you got a head start on the rest of us."

"We spent some time at the Happy Valley Canteen," he says. "Up by K-25. I tell you what---Happy Valley's got anything you want. And I do mean anything!" He's trying to buddy up to Marcus, who isn't the least bit interested.

Marcus sips his coffee. "Got to get up there sometime."

"That's where Dorothy used to hang out," Eddie says. "You're okay with me talking about her, right? I know you're seeing a lot of her these days." Marcus wonders, *What's he mean by "seeing a lot of her?"* Marcus doesn't give much stock to coincidences, and Eddie always seems to be talking about Dot when she's not around. *What does Eddie know that I don't?*

Eddie's a funny guy. Not funny ha ha. Funny smart ass. A tough guy who's pure country. You can tell by the way he talks. Pore white trash talk. And Eddie's got a distinctive aroma to him. Like he's worn the same leather jacket way too long. Nobody else says anything about it, but everybody notices. From what Marcus has seen sometimes Eddie's content to sit on the sidelines when others are hollering. He loves to pick at you. When he walks in, the place quiets down. Marcus doesn't tangle with him, but he plays his hand straight out like he would with anybody. Not hostile, not antagonizing, but down the middle. Nobody else does that with Eddie.

Dot used to be with him, and Marcus is still perplexed about what she saw in Eddie. *Saw*, as in past tense. Marcus doesn't trust Eddie any further than he can throw him. But here's Eddie clapping his hand around Marcus's shoulders with a roguish grin. Friendly as can be. "Good buddy, can I ask a favor?"

"Ask away."

"In about a hour can you give me a ride back up to Happy Valley?"

"Won't be here that long, but I can give you a ride in five minutes."

Not what Eddie wants to hear. "Let me check around. If I need you, I'll be back." And Eddie moves away, surveying the room. Marcus watches Carlotta tending to the couple that moved across the dining room, and she catches sight of Eddie. If looks could kill, Eddie's dead and buried. The other boys are still loud and rowdy, but Eddie isn't mixed up with them now. Carlotta's going after Eddie when he isn't really the problem. Not now anyway.

She's breathing fire, huffing at him more than the others. "You all need to quiet down. This is a respectable place. I aim to keep it that way."

Eddie handles her. "Yes'm. I hear you. I'll take care of it." Sounding reasonable.

Eddie goes over to his buddies, his voice not so loud, hushing them, getting them to listen. He puts an arm around Reggie's shoulders, grinning at the others. They glance at Carlotta, who's still stern returning to the counter to pick up ready dishes. In five minutes the loud crew's gone, and Eddie the peacemaker has come to sit by Marcus again. He says, "I told them go to the Clock Alley in Happy Valley. They're hot to trot, if you know what I mean."

Eventually, Marcus agrees to take Eddie where he wants to go. He's rethinking Eddie, not exactly giving him the benefit of the doubt, just keeping an open mind. Eddie won't ever be his good buddy. Not even close. This hard-boiled fellow's half fox, half snake. But maybe he's something else, too.

They've gone a couple of blocks when Eddie sighs like he's quit holding his breath, fidgeting a little, and he says, "Change of plans, Brummett. Can you stop off at the hospital?" Eddie's lost his joviality. "Just let me off in the front. Main door. When I'm done, I can catch the bus to K-25. Then walk to the hutment. Unless you can come back to get me." Eddie opens up a little bit, talking in a way he wouldn't with his rowdy buddies. Not egging anybody on now. Actually asking for help. "I need to get a shot and checked. No big thing. It's a little messy is all. That's what the doc tells me."

The hospital's an expansive, two-story, wood frame structure. Eddie hops out a little stiffly, sticking his head back in the window. "Appreciate the ride. I'd ask you not to mention where you've dropped me off. The gang I was with, they'd never let me hear the last of it." He sounds grateful and embarrassed at the same time, not slinking, not instigating.

Marcus says, "You going to be all right then?"

Eddie chuckles grimly. "Depends on what the doc says. I might need to wait a while. An hour or so."

Standing there, Eddie doesn't look too good. When he turns to walk away he looks worse. A slight limp altering his gait as he heads toward the front doors. Can't tell which leg's hurting the man, if that's what it is.

Out of curiosity Marcus goes out Louisiana Avenue toward Happy Valley. The place has streets laid out in a grid, mostly numbered streets, not named after states, row after row of brand new hutments and then the J. A. Jones Trailer Camp, dozens of trailers crammed close together. Lots of red mud all over. No plumbing in the hutments or trailers. Communal washhouses. It's like a muddy frontier camp unto itself.

He locates the Canteen easily, a crowd of carousing men moiling around, agitated and belligerent, some obviously drunk. A few females attracting lots of male attention. Most of them look like they can stand honky tonk goings-on and one-night stands that usually go with it. Satisfied Eddie was right on about Happy Valley, Marcus wants to see about Dot. But probably best to start with Carlotta. Find out where Dot's staying. Go see her. Should have done that already. *Why haven't I done that?*

He goes back to the Guest House, heads to his room, strips down to undershirt and shorts, lies on his cot, hands behind his head, trying to settle in. Settle down if he can. But something's not right. He's not sure what it is. Something about Dot dating Eddie a while ago.

He's restless, aimless, unfocused. His mind comes back to the plague Wells mentioned. *What's that about?* Just thinking about it stirs him up.

In five minutes he's dressed, backing the coupe out of the lot. He goes by the Café first. No luck. Not knowing why, he heads to the Hospital which is all lit up, but pretty quiet as he walks inside and up to the nurse at Reception. "I dropped a guy off here about an hour ago. Said he needed to see a doctor. Did you see him?"

"Name?"

"Eddie. Don't know his last name."

"Which doctor?"

"He didn't say."

Exasperated, she says, "Good friend of yours, is he?" She gives him the side eye. It's nearly 2300 hours. She must be tired.

"Listen," Marcus says. "He's good looking. Hair's slicked back, sort of wavy. Looks a little bit like Dana Andrews. It would be great if you can remember you saw him come in, especially if you know which doctor saw him." Then he remembers. "He's got a slight limp. Walks slow." Realizing that walking slow applies to him, too, sometimes.

The nurse looks him over, deciding what to say. He figures she's hesitating answering because she saw where Eddie went.

"Dr. Burgess has three patients waiting," she says. "Your friend could be one of them."

"Can I see him?"

"Burgess is with Dr. Cadwallader, head of the Hospital, working late tonight. You don't want to get in between those two. Don't bother them."

"I meant see Eddie."

"Burgess is the one to decide that. I'll call his nurse. Let her know about you. Wait over there if you want." She's pointing to wooden chairs lined up against the opposite wall.

Marcus takes a seat, and, after a minute when he hears approaching footsteps, stands up to speak to whoever it is. A janitor pushing a rolling trash cart. Marcus sits back down. There's noise, indistinct voices, doors closing down the hall. He's more than ready to see Burgess, but he asks where he can use a phone, and the nurse says, "Right here if it's a brief call."

He calls the front desk at the Guest House. They don't have anything for him.

Minutes later two doctors in their white coats and a civilian...a young guy who looks like he's still in high school, skinny, wearing glasses...The three of them come down the hall. There's a female with them, tall, slender. He knows her---Trudy Allistair. She's listening intently to one of the doctors, doesn't see Marcus standing there. No one's aware of him.

One of the White Coats answers, but his voice is too low for Marcus to make out what's said. The taller doctor wears his hair a little too long for military. The other doctor's older, wears glasses, not as tall as Trudy, but he's military for sure.

"The bloody discharge is to be expected," the square-faced fellow tells Trudy. "She'll be all right if she takes the medicine prescribed. Of course, no intimacy for a week to ten days. She'll know when she's getting better. The discomfort will have diminished."

Trudy's scowling. She says, "I'm her step-sister, My mother married her Dad. I'm making sure she gets what she needs. Just looking after my sister."

The older doctor looks to his colleague before answering. "The medicine she needs is either mercury, arsenic, or sulfur. Diluted, of course, just light doses for seven days' time. We've given her 1000 milligrams of bismuth just now. We use a cocktail of varying proportions, depending on the patient."

The shorter doctor adds, "She needs to abstain in the meantime. And, of course, inform her partner."

Trudy laughs harshly, "He's the one that told her. And let me tell you, Bea was crushed. Just crushed." As she says this she notices Marcus, and he gets the idea seeing him will cause a problem, but it doesn't. She takes her leave from the doctors and comes over to him. "You here about Bea?" Then she does a double take. "No, how could you be? She hasn't told anybody but me."

"She sick?"

Trudy's fiddles in her purse for something. A cigarette. "Come outside, and I'll explain. She's not sick, not really."

They drift over to the coupe to sit in the front seat. In no hurry she's inhaling deeply. He's not a smoker. Neither is Groves, so he gets the windows run all the way down. "Trying to keep the smoke out of the car."

"Let's get back out then," she says, "and I'll tell you what I know. I don't know everything, mind you. Just what Bea's told me after I pushed her on it. She's crying her heart out."

"About what?"

"Let's just say it's a female problem." She gives him the eye to see if he gets the implications. When he stays quiet, she says, "You heard what the doctors said, didn't you?"

"Some. Just a little bit. She's bleeding?"

Trudy nods. "Yep, she got hurt all right, but not in the way you're talking about."

He shakes his head, remembering about the transfusions and the rest of it. "Just what the hell are we talking about?" he says with more tension in his voice than's intended.

Bitterly, Trudy says. "Whatever' she got, I expect it's called a lot of different things. But that doesn't matter. She knows how she got it…who she got it from. My sister's not real experienced. Shoot! This bastard that gave this to her might be first guy she's actually gone out with. You know, alone." She tosses the cigarette on the ground, rummaging for another. "Let me do this one, and I'll be ready to go back inside."

When Marcus was stationed in South Carolina he saw guys afflicted sort of like Bea Moynihan. They didn't brag about it, but there was a kind of twisted male pride for catching it. After all, it was proof positive you'd done the deed. You'd found the promised land at least once. And the medics could take care of you if they caught it early. It could get worse fast though if you hid it. Bad news if you didn't get medicated in time. Marcus didn't think about it much.

He'd never been with a girl who had it, so he didn't know the worst parts.

Trudy says, "Bea's older than me by three and a half years, but in some ways she's just a baby. Doesn't paint her face. And she's not so agile dealing with the kind of guy who takes advantage. Apparently, she let some bastard take her wherever he wanted her to go." Smoke drifts over her head. Then she looks at Marcus. "What you doing here anyway? You got it, too?" She laughs coarsely.

"I brought a guy here. Promised to take him up to Happy Valley, but he needed to stop off here."

"So why're you hanging around? You must have something else going on."

"Listen," he says, "I can take you two where you want to go. No problem. You two stay in a dorm?"

"Oh, would you? That'd be great. We stay at Davenport Hall," she says. "Let me get Bea."

They go back in, and Trudy heads down the hall, but turns to him. "Why don't you go back out? Pull up right in front of the main door. I'll bring her out. Just take your cue from me."

He's heading out, but remembers the receptionist. Goes over to her and says, "If Eddie comes out before I get back, tell him I'll be back in a half hour or so. I can drive him back to his place."

"Okay," she says. "What's your name anyway?"

He tells her and heads outside. After a couple minutes Trudy brings her sister to the idling coupe. No one's talking, Marcus staring straight ahead as they get into the backseat. He heads out, aiming for Davenport Hall. Beatrice Moynihan is subdued, trying to disappear. Every now and then he hears her sniffling. He sneaks glances in his rearview mirror. Trudy's murmuring to her, rubbing Bea's arm, patting her shoulder. It takes seven minutes to get to Davenport.

Trudy almost carries Moynihan up the steps into the hall at Davenport. It's like all the other dorms Marcus has been in, an H-shaped building two stories high, long halls, room after room after room. Sleeping quarters for women only. When they reach the front door, Trudy turns halfway around, still supporting her sister. "See you later." That's all there is to it.

Marcus sits in the coupe a while. It's a dark, cloudy night, but he can smell smoke from burning brush somewhere west of the hospital. He's trying to connect the dots. Trudy, Moynihan, Eddie What's-His-Name. He goes a little further: Carlotta and Dot. Finally, there's the General. He sorts all of them and goes back. With thoughts of Dot Swicegood from quiet, little Sweetwater, Tennessee, a couple hours or so down the road.

All this is rolling around in his head, and he gets the idea it's best to head to the Guest House. It's after midnight. But Groves is out of town and won't be back for a few days. Can't remember exactly when he's due back, but it's not tomorrow, that's for sure. Or is it? Marcus realizes he's not a hundred percent sure. He's undone. Something's nagging at him. Not Groves. *What is it?*

Davenport Hall's west of Grove Center, which itself is west of the Guest House. The Hospital's between Marcus and his bed, so that makes it easy. If Dot started feeling worse than Carlotta said, maybe she saw a doctor. Maybe he should check the hospital. He decides to stop back there. He recognizes that some of what he's feeling is jealousy or at least envy. Some of it's about Eddie and Dot before Marcus found her. He wants to talk to somebody…probably Dot first. Then maybe Carlotta or Trudy. He realizes all this is screwed up, but, if he can find Dot, it'll be worth this roaming around. His mother would tell him, "You're acting a fool about this girl you're chasing after. Are you sure about her?"

Not really sure. But he's set on her. Not inclined to let her go.

Happy Valley

Marcus parks out front of the hospital, and he's nearly to the door when Eddie emerges. "Hey, Brummett. We still going to Happy Valley? You got to get up there. That place never sleeps. Never quits."

Marcus says, "Yeah, I can take you." He figures Eddie must have got good news from his doctor. Seems like he doesn't have a care in the world. He's a Good Time Charlie.

Eddie's much relieved. "How about I buy you a beer?" He's genuinely friendly.

The first cold beer goes down real easy. He doesn't object when Eddie gets him a second, then gets a third. Marcus doesn't know any of the people who've joined them. They've pushed three tables together. It's smoky, and it's getting rowdy, everybody paired up with someone of the opposite sex except Marcus. A lot of noise, most of them not listening much to one another.

Laughing, drinking, everybody feeling no pain. Couples hanging onto each other like long lost lovers who've just found each other, drifting into the shadows or out the door. Wanton, randy impulses all around. At the table all manner of lies are told. Marcus can tell because while he's sipping his Old Milwaukee the guys are telling and retelling the same stories, forgetting some of the details they laughed about ten minutes ago.

Marcus feels pretty mellow, but by 0230 hours his hip pains him, and he realizes he's wasting time here. Got to limber up and find Dot. He backtracks all through the Townsite, beginning with the Central Bus Terminal, checking the buses that have come in. Then the Café. Nothing going on there, so he's back in the coupe, without any new strategy, just an anxious wanderlust. He goes by K-25, too, and Y-12 with nothing to show for it. Pointless. Driving just to be driving. He's motivating on a full tank of gas. There's nobody to talk to; and it's nearly 0300 hours, very dark. And before he's ready he finds himself going through Solway Gate, heading into quiet country. Dark and foggy this close to the river. After a few minutes with no traffic on the road he comes up on about a dozen deer traipsing across the road, eyes bright gold in his headlights, silent, dainty steps. And gone.

He sees signs for several Tennessee towns further south, Philadelphia, Athens, Cleveland, and Sweetwater, which is about 65 miles away. He doesn't care about the other towns. He's going to Sweetwater.

That's all he needs. Doesn't matter how long it'll take. Doesn't matter if the whole thing's foolish in the extreme.

It takes nearly an hour and a half to reach Sweetwater, and at Biggs Street there's an Esso station. B & B's Place. Lights on. Pickup truck parked at the side of the building.

He parks out front and walks up to the door, peering through the plate glass window, looking for someone to talk to. There's a section of dining tables and chairs on one side with aisles of shelved goods on the other side. He hears indistinct voices somewhere in the back. As he's straining to make out what's being said, three figures emerge, two middle-aged women and an elderly man coming out from a back room, obviously surprised to see him.

"Hello, folks," he says loud enough so they can hear through the glass. "Is there a phone I can use? I got to make a call." He reaches for his wallet. "I can pay."

The women wear aprons, hairnets, and rubber gloves, most likely fixing breakfast from scratch. This place does more than sell gas. Combination general store and eating place for early risers. He glances at his watch: it's 0520. Eastern sky beginning to glow. The women look to the man who says, "Come set a spell, young fella." He unlocks the front door, offering a mischievous smile. "Why you got to wake somebody up with a dang telephone call before six A.M.? And just who are you anyway?" Marcus introduces himself. They shake.

This old fellow's shorter than the women, who resemble one another. They don't have a rough, oversized nose like he does. Sisters maybe? He's older by twenty years or so, maybe their father. He's wearing a slouch hat and overalls. Muddy brogans. Pot belly flowing over his belt. He says, "We're the Brakebill family." He gestures to the women. "I'm William Brakebill, their uncle, and we're getting ready for the breakfast crowd. I got to unlock the gas pumps first. You set here. We'll talk a bit." He squeezes out the door for the pumps, directing his nieces, "Get back to work, ladies." Which they do, leaving Marcus waiting.

Brakebill is uncle to Mrs. Holtzclaw and Miss Dean, who brings them coffee at the largest table in the place. Brakebill is loving the sound of his own voice while the women are more like church mice, almost noiseless in the kitchen. Now and then one peeks around a corner at them. Brakebill's holding court in the dining room for a party of two.

The coffee's good and steaming, and it helps Marcus recall he hasn't eaten since 1700 hours yesterday. His stomach growls at him. Brakeville turns halfway round in his chair, calling to the kitchen, "Lorene, Gladys, bring us biscuits. Or cornbread. I'd like cornbread myself." He turns back to Marcus. "You?"

"Either one's fine," he says.

Lorene delivers a hot plateful of both, and the men have some of each with butter and Karo. Brakebill interrogates Marcus, learning he's a sergeant originally from Newport News, Virginia, assigned to drive an officer around the base in Anderson County. And that car out front's the one he drives.

"What base you talking about?" Brakebill says, buttering his third biscuit.

"The CEW…Clinton Engineer Works."

"In Anderson County you say? In Clinton?"

"No, sir. It's about eight miles from Clinton."

"Don't know it."

Brakebill snaps his fingers, gets up, and goes over to the cash register. "Let me look it up," he says, opening a drawer, bringing out a folded state map, which he spreads out to get his bearings. After a minute he folds the map back up. "Don't see it here."

"It's new. Might not be on any map," Marcus says, realizing this could generate more questions.

Brakebill frowns. "Well, shit fire. Not on any map you say?" And he scowls at the next piece of cornbread as he drowns it in syrup. "What kind of place is this CEW outfit you're talking about?"

"Well, they don't tell you much about what's going on there, but it's safe to say it's about the War Effort. They got welders and plumbers, electricians and machinists everywhere you look. Crews working every day of the week, eight-hour shifts all day, all night, going at it fast and furious."

Brakebill gives a low whistle, shaking his head. "I see that nice auto you got. I expect you know more than you're letting on."

Marcus smiles, but that's all.

After a while like that Brakebill says, "What's brung you to us here in Monroe County in the dead of night?"

"Mr. Brakebill, can I use the phone first? I got to check in on my boss. He might want me to come pick him up. He's unpredictable that way."

"Sounds like a long-haired, powered joe. But he probably ain't great shakes because you're playing fast and loose just being here so far from Clinton."

Marcus offers another brief grin, understanding how foolish he's looking. "You could say that, I guess."

"Does your boss man know you're in Sweetwater? Ain't nothing shaking around here. Not that the Army would want to know about." Brakebill pushes back from the table, stretches his legs out in front of him, settling in, taking his time observing his guest.

Marcus doesn't want to be studied very long, so he brings out his wallet. "It'll be a long distance call I need to make, but I can pay for it. And my biscuits, too." He hands the man two dollars, which will be more than enough. Brakebill smooths out the bills, slides them into a pocket. "Go ahead then. Don't mind me."

It's behind the counter. Marcus decides to call the Café to get Carlotta, if she's there. It's early, but she does baking on Thursdays, starting before the place opens up. He'll ask about Dot. Surely, she can tell him something. Should have done this before, but it was too early to get anybody on the phone. Then he can call the Guest House.

Marcus doesn't want Brakebill or his nieces overhearing him, but privacy's anything but a sure thing. He dials the number for the Café, but nothing happens. He does this three separate times. Nothing happens, so he gets the operator, who takes her own sweet time answering. "How can I help you?"

"I need to connect with Central Bus Terminal Café in the CEW. The Clinton Engineer Works. I've dialed. It's not going through."

"Is that in Clinton?"

"Well, no, but it's close."

Clicking sounds and static. Then "You'll have to be more specific, sir. I see no listing for a Bus Terminal Café in Clinton."

"Not in Clinton. Eight miles or so from Clinton. Can you please try again?"

This time silence lasts a minute or two. "Sorry, sir. No Clinton Engineer Works listed. No such place in our directory."

"Hmm. Well, can you connect me with the Guest House…also in the CEW?"

Static and then, "No, sir. I don't see a Guest House either. Don't know about any Clinton Engineer Works." He can hear a little petulant edge in her voice. He signs off and returns to the table, frustrated, but also ready to get something done. His eyes are scratchy with fatigue, but he's hell bent to get on the road. When he's back at the Café he can talk to Carlotta face-to-face. Then he can check on Groves, too. He's come this far. He wants to see where Dot has come from. He needs some more of that good coffee, too. Strong stuff to keep alert.

"No luck?" Brakebill asks.

"None," he says, reaching for his coffee. Brakebill hollers for Gladys to bring more, which is just what Marcus needs. He says, "Listen, I appreciate your letting me use the phone. And thanks for the breakfast. I'm going to see if I can find the Swicegood place. I've come this far. I ought to take a look. Then I need to head back." All this sounds jumbled up and foolish, but that's it. That's what he wants to do.

Brakebill perks up. "You're seeking Swicegoods you say? Gladys said you was. Why didn't you tell me earlier? Verla Swicegood runs a good-sized Victory Garden with Gladys. So my niece will know about them. I believe she goes to church with Swicegoods, too, down at First Baptist. I'm a Methodist man myself." He turns again to call out, "Gladys, come talk to Sgt. Brummett about the Swicegoods."

The younger woman comes around the corner, an inquisitive look on her face, wide-eyed as she approaches the table, rubbing flour off her hands.

Brakebill says, "Gladys, tell about the Swicegoods. He's come looking for Dorothy. Is she home? Do you know?" Still seated, he puts an arm around her waist, hugging her closer. Enjoying himself. "Tell the man what you know."

Gladys blushes at her collar and cheeks, but she nods a couple times before asking, "How do you know Dorothy? Do you work with her?"

"No. Only known her about a month, but I sure do think a lot of her. She's a peach."

Gladys seems skeptical, squinting at him.

"Let me tell you a few things that will help," he says. "She's changed jobs recently. Used to work at a place they call Y-12. But she left there. Now she's waiting tables. She has a real good friend named Carlotta." He wants them to understand he really knows

Dot. He looks back at Gladys a long moment. She's the one deciding whether to tell about Dot, not Brakebill. "Does what I've told you, does it fit her? I told her I'd like to see her homeplace." This is a little bit of a lie, but it might help.

Gladys moves away from the table a few steps, rubbing her face, staring at the kitchen. "Let me talk with Lorene."

She goes to do that, and Brakebill chuckles a bit. "The ladies nearly always got to do things together. But Dorothy Swicegood doesn't always make it easy on you. Know what I mean?"

"She can flare up feisty, that's for sure," Marcus says, not letting on how he likes her feisty. When she shows a little spark.

Brakebill chuckles again. "I believe you know Dorothy Swicegood as well as I do. I sure believe you do. Sweet on her are you?"

Marcus nods. "She's awful nice."

"Pretty as a picture, too," Brakebill says, grinning again. "I don't blame you one iota. I wish you good luck with her." He half turns in his chair, calling out, "Ladies, Sergeant Brummett, he's got to be getting back. Come on out here to clue us in on things."

Lorene comes out ahead of Gladys, seemingly more comfortable than her sister. She walks right up to Brakebill. "Hold your horses, Uncle Bill. Gladys told me what you're talking about, and I know Verla pretty good. She's not home. She and the boys are helping their cousin Malcolm down in Niota this week. Won't be back til Sunday afternoon. Dorothy's come a couple times to visit the home folks, but she ain't home now. Somebody might be there, but not Dorothy." She rubs her chin, adding, "I heard her daddy's in the South Pacific."

Brakebill says, "That's right, that's right. Malcolm's running a bulldozer on some godforsaken island. He left Sweetwater a month after Pearl Harbor. Verla's farming and raising three little boys. Has helped out her cousin now and then. And Malcolm's helped her out when she needed it. Good family. Fine lady."

Marcus takes that in for a minute. He says, "Could I use the phone to call the Swicegood place? Maybe Miz Swicegood's back home. I'd like to meet her. Do you think she's an early riser? Like you all? I might be waking her up."

Gladys says, "They don't have a phone."

Brakebill looks to Marcus. "That's right," he says. "Lots of Sweetwater families without phones. They use my counter phone just like you did."

"Well, shoot!" Marcus says. "I'm snakebit."

Lorene says, "They don't live too far away. I can tell you how to go, make you a map so you can come back when Dorothy's home sometime. How's that?"

Marcus studies their faces. Brakebill says, "Best we can do today, son."

So Marcus shakes their hands. "I appreciate it. And, ladies, you make a awful good biscuit. I'll be coming back to see you sometime."

Lorene scurries to the counter, locates scratch paper in the drawer, bringing out the folded map. Brakebill's hitching up his trousers, eyeing the cornbread and biscuits. "You paid too much for the biscuits, son. We'll give you a couple free and clear next time." And that's how it ends up as Marcus goes back out to the coupe.

Now at 0620 hours he's following Lorene's map, headed just two miles west through pastures along with fields of potatoes, corn, and milo. Dot had talked about the milo, saying, "Milo was Verla's latest brainstorm. She's got a powerful intuition about her. Can't always tell you why she wants something, but she's nearly always right. We been getting good prices for the milo." She gave him a straight on look. "You need to come see my Momma sometime."

And that makes him feel pretty god about traveling to Sweetwater, Tennessee. Not sure he knows why he's so smitten by Dot Swicegood. He is, though.

After a while he finds the Swicegood place, an unpainted clapboard house with a porch across the front and what looks like a pump house plus a ramshackle barn out back. Crops set fairly close to the house. No vehicle out front. No sign of life. A hardscrabble place. He parks out in the yard where the ruts have led him. Getting out, climbing three porch steps, he knocks loud on the door and then wanders along, looking in windows. Is there any trace of Dot in these rooms? Hers alone, not her brothers, not her momma? A dark intuition is swelling up inside him about her, especially now he's seeing her home. He can almost taste what it would be like to be with Dot for a long, long time. Doing whatever it'll take to make her happy.

I can do that. I'll never stop doing it.

He likes the sound of that. Wonders if it's possible. But it can't be dwelt on just now because it's time to go. He realizes he needs to make tracks to the CEW. To check in with the Front Desk, be ready to deliver Groves wherever The Man says to go. That is, if he's back. But he'd rather find Dot, tell her how he feels.

The drive back goes a little quicker because the sun's brightening the fields on either side of the road, cattle herded together near the ponds and feeding troughs. Brighter, too, is the route itself with traffic going steady in both directions on this public road, not the road he knew so private last night. Along the way, he recalls he'll reach the Bus Terminal and the Café before he gets near the Guest House. So he might be able to save time, using Carlotta's phone to touch base with the Front Desk. Find out about Groves. Then find out about Dot. He feels like a message himself coming on the wind. Yet his time has got stuck, turned over on its side.

He crosses back into the CEW at Solway, which is jammed with traffic. A long line of Knoxville cars and buses stretches to the bridge and on to the Security Gate, where it slows down as the guards check each vehicle. There's two entrance lanes, but there's a multitude of cars in stop-and-go attitude. The opposite lane heading for Knoxville isn't as full, but that doesn't help. Sitting still so often makes him sleepy, but he shakes that off as much as he can.

He makes it to the Central Bus Terminal by 0750 hours, and, as he's hurrying across the parking lot, he does like always---assumes the worst. Groves will be fit to be tied, angry as a wet hen about not hearing from his driver. Marcus can hear him grumble, "We've got places to go, Sergeant. I need someone reliable. Someone I can depend on." Marcus hopes the General will get loud and indignant because, if that happens, him letting off steam, all in a rush, then he's likely to start thinking about where he's going next. Likely to forget about getting started late one morning, especially if Marcus makes all the right turns. But, if the General stays quiet and calm, that's bad. That might spell the end of Sergeant Marcus Brummett, the driver.

Then his mind jumps to Trudy and Carlotta, assuming the best. He'd like to bring those two together. Good people, the kind of friends who'll watch out for you. Both qualified in their own special way. Others might not see them that way, but he sure does because they've doled out unexpected kindness to him. Dot doesn't know Trudy, but he's confident he could explain about how Trudy took care of Moynihan at the hospital, and Carlotta would probably relate to that. He should have told Carlotta he was going to Sweetwater, but she wasn't there to tell, was she?

Then, as he's opening the Café door, he's ashamed he hasn't been in touch with any of these females to let them know what he's done, where he's gone. Not that it's important to them. Not like it is to him. Whatever's come over Dot doesn't matter. If she's got a problem, he'll take it on with her. He doesn't want to kiss Dot good-bye. He wants to kiss her goodnight. Every night for a lifetime. He's dwelling on that as he steps inside, searching for Carlotta.

His heart leaps up as he discovers Dot's there. But he's walked into something odd. She's out of breath, red-faced, fuming at someone. He can't tell who. There's a crowd for breakfast.

Dot is seething, wiping at her eyes, glaring fiercely. "She told me not to let you in here. Not to let you eat or sit or talk or anything. Get out! You hear me? Get out of my sight!"

The fellow she's addressing's stuck in place. It's Eddie. She's screeching at him, but he's calm, not reacting other than to show the sly, amused smirk he summons so easily. He shifts a little from one foot to the other, turning slightly to look around at his audience, and you can tell he's about to come back at her. That's what he's known for. Guys at two of the nearest tables sit up straighter, watching and listening. Their eyes are full of *This ought to be good.*

Though he doesn't know how this started, Marcus knows Eddie can take full advantage. This is what fox and snake live for. Dot's still worked up, unaware of him. Unconcerned with how everyone's watching. The whole place is silent except for her rapid breathing. He's never seen her this way. This fired up. Quickly, he searches for Carlotta. *Shouldn't she be handling this?*

Dot grabs a fork from one of the tables, brandishes it. Eddie holds up both hands, palms forward. "Whoa, whoa, whoa." He backs up a step.

"I told you to get out, didn't I?" Her voice seething, bitter.

Eddie turns a little more so he notices Marcus, and the smirk begins to slip away. Dot notices, too, but nothing changes for her.

Marcus steps up. "Better scram, Eddie. Someone's going to call the MP's if this gets any worse." Then an idea comes to him, and he calls out to the kitchen, "Carlotta, wait. Trouble's almost over."

Eddie looks around and says, "Who's Carlotta?"

Marcus keeps his tone friendly. "She runs the place. Short and stocky. You've seen her."

Eddie looks every which way. "Don't see her."

"Her phone's in the kitchen," Marcus says.

Eddie gives Marcus a peculiar look, part doubt, part gratitude. Then he turns to Dot and the fork. He brings back half of the smirk, telling her, "You won't do much damage with that.".

"Try me."

Eddie waits half a beat before sauntering out the door, glancing back at Dot, then Marcus, as if nothing had happened, leaving Marcus wary.

Dot lays the fork back on the table in front of a fellow who doesn't look hungry now. Marcus approaches, and she folds just right into his arms, which lasts a good while, and finally he says, "Let's talk," leading her toward the kitchen. The dining room resumes its prattle. She tells the busboys, two high schoolers, to handle things a little while, and they nod, looking at one another self-consciously.

Marcus asks the cook, a round, red-faced fellow, "Can you give as a couple minutes here? We won't be long."

The guy says, "Sure. I need a cigarette anyway." After he's stepped out Marcus gets Dot to sit while they talk. He starts off asking about Carlotta. "Where is she?"

Dot lets out her breath as if she'd been holding her breath. "Her Momma's had a stroke. Yesterday. Carlotta had to go back to New Jersey. Couldn't wait."

They talk about Carlotta a while, and he's glad they'd started with her, not the stand-off just concluded. They're both beholden to Carlotta. Dot's color slowly returns to something like normal. Her eyes still have the sparkle of agitation, but she slows down gradually. He offers her what little he knows. "I've come by, but missed you a couple times. I was beginning to get worried. Carlotta told me you were feeling poorly."

"Oh, that," she says, dismissively. "I wasn't doing too well. She's right about that. But I'm better now. I probably ought to…." She's going to tell him something, but she's not quite ready, not just yet. She lowers her gaze.

He says, "Sounds kind of serious."

She paces across the room and back again. Sits and tells him what she'd seen the doctors for. It's something like what Eddie had to get a shot for. Not sure what the exact word the doctors use for it, and it probably hits women different from the way it does men. Doctors confirmed it's curable. Not deadly, but he knows she's struggling just bringing it up. He mulls that over, watching her face. She wipes at both eyes a couple times, a wet streak slipping down one cheek. She wipes it away with a sleeve.

"You okay?" he asks.

"If you are," she says. "I need to tell you a few more things about my…my condition. For one thing, it's practically gone."

"You taking medicine?"

"Finished two nights ago." She offers a thin smile. "I'm well now. That's what my doctor said." The smile quivers a bit.

"Good," he says, reaching for her. This clinch lasts longer. He breathes in as she breathes out, her scent entering him as his does her. He's in no hurry to let her go.

The cook hurries back in. "There's three MP's out front, saying they need to talk to you."

"Oh, god." She shudders..

Marcus says, "Let me go first." Not asking, telling.

The cook leads him back to the dining room to find the MP's, one older, shorter guy along with two younger, much larger guys, who look to the old guy for direction. Marcus says, "Listen, I think the situation here has been resolved." He explains, pointing out nobody struck anyone, no verbal threats made. Over and done in two minutes.

The old guy asks a few questions: who started it? What was the basic problem? Do you think there'll be more trouble? Marcus handles it all quietly, calm as he can. He doesn't want Dot to come out to talk unless he can talk to her first. The shorter MP asks a few customers what they knew, how it went down.

"It wasn't nothing much happened," a guy says. "We were hoping we'd see something, but we didn't. Not worth talking about really."

The old guy nods, turns to the younger guys. "Anything else you want to know here?"

"No, sir."

He tells them go back out and wait. When they've left, he motions Marcus to a vacant table near the kitchen and says, "That Ford coupe in the parking lot. Is that what you drive?"

"It is."

"General Groves, right?"

Uh oh. Marcus hesitates. He isn't ready for this.

The guy says, "We been working at Solway Security Gate the last couple months. I've seen you bring Groves through from Knoxville time and again. Right? That was you."

"You got most of it right," Marcus says, although he's not sure he should have said that.

The guy says, "Wouldn't want to get on the wrong side of Groves by mucking things up with his driver." The corners of his mouth turn up for about two seconds. Then he says, "You vouch for her that was standing that guy down?"

"I do."

"That's all we need then. We know him. You got to watch him close," the guy says, offering his hand. So they shake hands, and that's that.

Marcus lets out a long breath before returning to Dot, who's standing with the cook. Marcus says, "It's okay. They're gone." And even though he knows he needs to talk much more with Dot, he discovers his personal energy, his battery has about run down. Staying up all night can lead to that.

He thanks the cook. "Appreciate your letting us cool down in here," he says.

Cook nods. "Like I said, I needed a little break myself."

Marcus walks Dot back out to the counter where the busboys are trying to read their own handwriting for the choices just made by a couple at the counter. Dot takes the paper, reads, then says, "I can't make out half what's written here. Do it again so Cook will know what they want." Hearing her straighten them out is a good thing.

The boys balk at this, but go back as directed. Marcus says, "I'm bushed. Let me get some shut eye, and we can talk when you get off." This is definitely the way to go, which he hopes she will agree is best. Gives her time to get back to work. Distract herself after the run in with Eddie. Give Marcus time in the sack. She'll finish up around 1500 hours.

So that's what happens. Marcus checks with the Guest House. Groves won't be back for eight days. Then he goes to his quarters, his hip troubling him some, but about half a minute after his head touches the pillow he's gone.

Later when he picks Dot up, he takes her for a drive, ending up on the banks of the Clinch River. She gives him more information about her infection, when it started, when she was declared officially well, how to avoid reinfection. But she doesn't talk much more about that. She slides across the front seat, pulling his face to hers, giving him a lingering kiss, a mixture of gratitude and desire and something else he doesn't recognize, but wants more of.

"Are you okay with this? Still want to be with me?"

"Sure do," he says, and her quick smile is pure sparkle.

So in days to come Marcus thinks he knows all he needs to know, and he's pretty satisfied with how things are working out. The General is more predictable now, and he spends more time off the CEW. Marcus is a semi-regular transporting officers and their wives or dates to Clinton, Rockwood, and Lenoir City where enterprising citizens cater to Army personnel and construction workers and scientific types from all over the world. Dot's mellowing, warming up to him again, affectionate like before, but there are times when she's noticeably down, and that worries him more often than he would like.

One night she kisses him better than just, "Hello, there, fella." He wonders what that was for, and a few minutes later she says, "Marcus, I need to know something about that thing with Eddie."

"Tell you anything you want to know."

She looks tormented a second, but then she takes a deep breath and says, "I'll pay you back somehow. I swear I will. I can't be with you if I can't pay you back for what you did that day with Eddie and the MP's. Whether or not we end up together, I got to do right by you. I been sad too much."

"I'm a patient man. I can outwait the sadness. I'll help you do it, too."

Dot turns away, struggling for air, sniffling, wiping her eyes. After a moment, she turns around, sniffling again. "How much did you have to bribe the MP's? You know, to get me off from what I did. Threatening somebody. I could have been in big trouble for losing control."

"You did sort of blow up on him. But you owe me nothing, Dot. Not a thing, I swear. That lead MP knew me from when I drove into and out of Solway with my boss. He cut me some slack. Just walked away, believing me. I figure he didn't want to rock the boat with the Brass. I was lucky. Both of us were lucky."

She's quiet, her eyes looking past him, over his shoulder, like she's deciding something that will make a difference for the rest of their lives. Or maybe somehow she doesn't believe him. He can't figure out which way she'll go. Finally, she settles her gaze on his face. In his eyes. And she says, "You don't have to tell me the man you drive for. You don't have to give me secrets from your work. I can live without knowing that. But don't lie to me. I want you to be mine alone. No chasing skirts, not if we promise each other we'll be faithful, we'll be pristine, both of us, together for always."

He smiles broadly. "You can count on me, Miss Swicegood."

*****

Five years after the War, General Groves gives orders to obliterate a portion of the Clinton Engineer Works due to a catastrophic alignment of plagues, a unique calamity, perhaps nuclear, although that has not been confirmed. But most definitely venereal.

His order reads: "There is a pathogenic substance in the water or in the earth or in the various materials manufactured at K-25. The campus there is nearly contiguous to an area known as Happy Valley, where serious problems persist to this day, even after K-25 has been refitted for additional purpose. This sexual contagion our personnel endure is remarkably pervasive and pernicious, a growing pestilence in our midst.

"We hereby mandate all personnel be trained about the risks of failing to wear protective gear or adhere to sanitation and disinfecting protocols. Furthermore, we discourage close, personal fraternization while off duty or while present at assigned work stations. Leadership at every level shall develop procedures to neutralize or otherwise abate any contamination by toxic materials in situ at K-25.

Furthermore, analysis by scientific and military specialists does not condone any additional funding to sustain the Happy Valley community. No further inquiry will be made into the status of the scores of dormitories, trailers, hutments, or public spaces (such as but not limited to laundry, post office, communal washrooms, canteen, bowling alley, or any other various social gathering sites). Further investigation of these phenomena at Happy Valley is not necessary.

"I hereby order the immediate evacuation of personnel

as well as demolition of all structures

comprising the neighborhood

known as Happy Valley.

All this contaminated area must be demolished

and eradicated.

Burn all that remains to ashes.

Bury it deep."

The End